A GUIDE TO SOLVING A MURDER

A Finn and Briar Cozy Mystery Book #1

COURTNEY MCFARLIN

Chapter One

One of my favorite things to do, early in the morning, as the world is just waking up, is taking a walk in the woods that surround my little cabin. It's even better in the summer months when the air was still cool, but the sun kisses your skin with the promise of warmth coming later in the day. It's my quiet time, almost a meditation, that prepares me for the rest of the day. Rain or shine, snow or not, you'll find me and my two best friends, taking our usual loop in the forest.

One of those best friends, Finn, had just completed her off leash morning zoomie session, while the other, Briar, walked next to me, picking her way through the pine needles that littered the ground, her long plume of a tail waving gently. They'd come from the same place, the shelter in Collinsville, Colorado, my hometown, as an unlikely bonded pair that had surprised the shelter staff to no end.

The cat, Briar, was a dog person, and Finn, the border collie, was a cat person. When Finn had been picked up off the streets, a bedraggled pup they estimated was around four months old, Briar had taken to her immediately, refusing to leave the pup's side. Even now, a year after being adopted, they insisted on being together.

They looked remarkably similar, right down to their long black and white fur.

Finn stopped on the trail, looking back over her shoulder, and woofed softly at me, encouraging us to pick up the pace.

"We're coming, Finn. I'm sure you're hungry. You ran like the wind earlier."

Finn woofed again, giving me her patented silly grin, before heading down the trail. She never got too far in front of us, though, even off the leash. I glanced down at Briar and smiled as her eyes met mine.

"Want a lift? You've been walking for a while."

Briar gave me a little kitty shrug and hurried down the trail, leaving me to walk faster to catch up. I'd originally wanted to adopt a dog who could accompany me on the long hikes I organized as part of my business, Wild Peak Expeditions, and ended up with a border collie who seemed to never tire, and an adventure cat who loved to walk. I smiled as I followed them down the trail. I wouldn't change a thing.

Finn's sharp bark sounded, and my steps faltered as I rounded the curve that led to my cabin. She rarely barked, preferring to communicate in a range of soft woofing noises, so this was definitely odd. Visions of mountain lions, bears, and other dangers stampeded through my mind as I hustled to join them on my front porch. A man was standing there, giving both animals a wary look. A man I didn't recognize. He was dressed in a suit, and looked incredibly out of place.

A black sedan was parked behind my Land Rover, blocking it in the narrow drive. I offered a hesitant smile as the man edged back off the porch steps.

"Are you Tessa Windsor?"

"Yes. What's this about?"

"This is for you."

He handed over a large envelope, never taking his eyes off my pets. Briar moved forward, sniffing the man's shiny dress shoes as he shifted in place. Finn's tail, typically a metronome of joy that knocked over everything in sight, was still and held low. Worry danced up my spine as I took the envelope from him. Sure enough, my name was scrawled on the front of it in black marker.

He turned and walked back to the sedan without another word. I looked down at the envelope and back at him as he got in the car.

"Who are you?"

He slammed the door and fired up the engine. My hand automatically reached for Finn's head as he pulled out of the drive and headed down the road, disappearing around the curve that led to the main highway.

"Well, that was weird."

Finn whined and went up on her hind legs, sniffing the envelope. I looked back down the road and shrugged before opening my front door and motioning them inside.

"I wonder how long he was here," I said, staring at the envelope as I walked in behind them. "I hope he didn't come in here."

Finn sniffed the floor, as if she was worried about the same thing, but she didn't appear overly alarmed, so I relaxed a fraction and headed towards the small kitchenette at the back of my cabin.

"Alright, guys. Let's get you some breakfast."

I put the envelope on the counter and grabbed their bowls from the dish rack next to the sink. My little cabin was home, but it wasn't exactly the lap of luxury. No dishwasher or fancy kitchen appliances. It was big enough for the three of us, though, and a cozy place that had quickly become my refuge from the outside world.

I'd purchased it years ago, back when property prices were low. It wasn't big, really just an open space on the main floor with a loft above for my bedroom, but it suited me. Its location, tucked into the forest, while still only five minutes from town, also suited me. I'd never regretted my purchase.

I dished up their food, set the bowls down on the floor and stared at the envelope again, where it sat on the counter like a harbinger of doom. I drummed my fingers on the counter, wondering what it might hold.

"I don't think it would be a summons. No one wants to sue me. That I know of, anyway. There's no return address on it. Strange."

Smacking noises were the only response from Finn and Briar as they enjoyed their breakfast. I knew I needed to open the envelope, if only to appease my curiosity, but something held me back. Instead, I poured water in the coffee pot, added in a few scoops of coffee, and waited.

Finn finished her breakfast first, and like always, waited for her friend patiently. Briar was the fastidious one, taking time to lick every speck of food from her bowl. By the time the coffee was done, the cat had finally finished her meal and sat next to Finn, washing her face. I stared at the envelope again as I took my first sip of coffee. The rich, hazelnut flavored brew sparked my brain to life.

"All right. Let's open it and see what it says."

Briar leapt onto the counter and sniffed at the envelope, her green eyes bright. She pawed at it, putting tiny marks on the paper. I snagged it away from her and tore open the back flap.

One sheet of paper was inside, folded into thirds. Briar crowded close, her whiskers tickling my hand. Finn leaned against my leg, her solid warmth seeping through the thin fabric of my leggings.

The letterhead proclaimed that it had come from the law offices of Reginald Endicott, Esquire, a name I'd never heard or seen in my life. I squinted at the small type below his name and frowned.

"Huh, Welder, Colorado. I wonder where that is?"

Briar pawed at my hand and I kept reading, my voice loud in the quiet space of my kitchen.

"It says Dear Miss Windsor. It is with great sadness that I inform you of the passing of your great aunt Euphemia Hawthorne. Please present yourself at my office today, the fifteenth of July, by two in the afternoon, to collect your inheritance. If you do not arrive, all future claims to this inheritance shall be forfeit. Kind regards, Reginald Endicott, Esquire."

I trailed off and looked at Briar and then at Finn.

"I have a great aunt named Euphemia? Or had. This has to be a mistake. I've never heard of her in my life. Let me call this number."

I pulled my phone out of the side pocket on my leggings and squinted at the tiny print on the letterhead, finally making out the number of the attorney. I punched it in and waited. And waited some more while it rang and rang. No voicemail option. I ended the call and frowned.

"Well, this is just weird. I wonder if Paul got anything?"

My brother, Paul, ran the local newspaper in Collinsville. We'd become close over the past few years, after his divorce, and after our parents moved to Florida to escape the brutal mountain winters. He was four years older than me, and one of my best friends, despite being a pain-in-the-butt older brother sometimes.

Briar pawed at my phone, almost as if she knew what I was thinking, while Finn let out a low whine, her tail slowly wagging. They adored my brother, almost as much as they loved my other best friend, Meggie Dolan. Meggie probably won the competition, thanks to the fact she ran a restaurant in town, and always saved choice treats for my pets.

I dialed Paul's number and smiled when his voice hit my ear, growly from a lack of sleep, and probably his seasonal allergies.

"Do you know what time it is?"

I glanced at the microwave, wincing when I realized I'd neglected to reset the clock the last time we'd lost power, and shrugged, even though he couldn't see me.

"Morning?"

"Hardy-har. You know I was up late putting the paper to bed last night. I was just going back to sleep after some guy showed up at my apartment, banging on the door."

"Let me guess. Tall guy, mid-thirties, fancy suit and shiny black shoes?"

"That is oddly specific and extremely accurate. How..."

"He came here, too. Finn wasn't a big fan of the guy. He asked if I was Tessa Windsor and shoved an envelope at me before high-tailing it out of here. I assume he hit you up before he came out here?"

"He was here about thirty minutes ago, so that tracks. He did the same thing here. Did you open it yet?"

"Of course I did. Are you telling me you didn't?"

My brother was the most curious person I'd ever met. It served him well as the editor-in-chief and head reporter at the Collinsville

Clarion. Exhaustion had to be the only reason he hadn't given in to the urge to open it.

"Not yet. I'm guessing from your tone I need to?"

"Uh, yeah. I'll wait."

He grumbled into the phone, vowing retribution to be decided at a later date, and enacted when I least expected it, but I heard him open the envelope. He mumbled something I couldn't hear before clearing his throat and sneezing.

"We have a great aunt Euphemia?"

"I guess?"

"Huh."

"Yeah, that was pretty much my reaction. I called the number on the letterhead, but no one answered. So, are you going to go? You're off today, so you'll have time. I don't have any hikes scheduled for today, so I might as well go. We can carpool."

"Go? You think this is serious? It's gotta be a joke, Tess."

"Or maybe not. Maybe we'll be millionaires. Maybe Aunt Euphemia was one of those secretive hermits who lined the walls of her dilapidated mansion with dollar bills."

"Again, weirdly specific. You watch too many gothic mysteries."

"Hey, if you don't want to go, I'll just claim your share. That would serve you right."

He snorted before sneezing again. Briar's eyes widened with alarm at the explosive noise coming through the phone.

"Bless you. Have you taken your allergy medicine?"

"Yes. I always do. Does it help? No, it doesn't. I don't know why I bother. Every summer, this happens. I can barely go outside."

"Oh, poor baby. Do you need a tissue?"

He huffed a laugh and I could almost see him shaking his head through the phone. His hair, dark blond like mine, standing on end from where he'd run his fingers through it.

"I'll be fine. You know what, let's do it. Like you said, we're both off today. It's probably a hoax, but what the heck? I'd hate to give up something and never know what I missed out on."

"I knew I could count on you and your curiosity. I'll pick you up."

"Where are we going?"

"Welder. I don't even know where that is. I hope it's not on the other side of the state. We might not make it in time."

"Lemme look. One second..."

He dropped the phone, letting out a few choice words, and I waited patiently as I poured myself another cup of coffee. Finn headed into the living room, where she hopped on the couch and settled down with a contented groan. Briar stayed on the counter, her eyes glued to mine.

"It's about an hour away from here, on the border with Wyoming. Looks like a tiny little town."

"So, we need to be there at two. We should leave here by noon, just in case. I don't want to get lost."

"If you'd let me drive, we wouldn't get lost. You're an ace on the trails, Tess, but my gosh, get you behind the wheel and all bets are off."

I narrowed my eyes and put my cup on the counter.

"Take that back. I'm an excellent driver."

"Ha. Well, it's nine now. So that means I can get a few hours of sleep before we leave. I don't think there's any place to eat in Welder, so we should grab lunch before we go."

"I'll bring sandwiches. Go get some sleep. We'll pick you up at noon."

His only answer was a loud yawn, and I laughed as I ended the call. I ruffled Briar's fur and finished the last of my coffee.

"Well, looks like our relaxing afternoon is postponed, guys. But hey, road trip!"

Finn's ears perked up, and she raised her head, a doggy smile firmly in place. The only thing she loved more than running was going for a ride. Briar tolerated it, usually claiming the back seat and stretching out while Finn sat in front, staring at everything we passed.

I rinsed out my mug, cleaned their bowls, and left everything to dry on the rack before heading up to my loft to get ready. I sincerely doubted the letter was real, but a tiny part of me was truly excited.

Chapter Two

After trying (and failing) to keep myself amused for two hours, all the while wondering about this mysterious great aunt of mine, I finally gave up. I packed two lunches and some snacks for Finn and Briar and headed out to my vehicle. I held open the back door for Briar while Finn circled my legs, panting with excitement.

"Okay, you can ride up front with me, but you'll have to move into the back when we pick up Paul."

She tilted her head to the side, brown eyes full of mischief, and I laughed as I opened my door and she vaulted inside, sailing over the seat. She turned around three times and stared out the window.

I stowed the lunch cooler in the backseat with Briar and got settled into the driver's seat. As soon as I turned the engine over, Finn shifted in her seat, wiggling with anticipation as I backed down the narrow drive. I rolled the window down and she stuck her nose out, lungs filling with air like a pair of bellows.

"All right, guys. Let's head to the office and double check things before we get Paul."

My little office was in the same building as Paul's newspaper, tucked onto the side with a separate entrance. When Paul bought the newspaper, he'd insisted on renovating the extra office space to house my expedition business, earning my eternal gratitude. Before that, I'd attempted to run the business from my home, but I was too far off the beaten path to convince people to make the trip.

Now, when people wanted to book a hike, they could conveniently find me right downtown, and the office was big enough to display the brochures I'd had printed up for the various hikes I offered. I'd been surprised by the amount of foot traffic I'd received since making the switch, and business was booming.

I pulled into the alley and parked, leaving the AC on for Finn and Briar.

"I'll be right back."

The heat smacked me in the face once I opened my door. Even though the morning had been nice and cool, even a little chilly, it was shaping up to be a scorcher. I unlocked the front door and went inside, flipping on the light, grateful I hadn't scheduled a hike for the day. Even though it would be cooler up in the mountains, I'd learned the hard way that warm weather hikes weren't great for customers, who invariably never listened to my recommendations to pack enough water to keep from getting dehydrated.

I sat in my chair and spun around in a circle before flipping on my computer to check my email. Sure, I could do it on my phone, but there was something special about having a place to go to do my actual work and I'd practiced separating my home life from my business, after learning, once again, the hard way about work/life balance.

I glanced at the clock above the door and quickly sorted through my email. Five new bookings had come in and it looked like the rest of the week was going to be busy. I turned off my computer and headed back outside, scurrying to get back inside the cool interior of my car.

"Let's go get Paul, guys."

My brother's apartment was just a few blocks from the newspaper office, and surprisingly, he was waiting outside, leaning against the main entry door, when I pulled in. A smile that might have been a little wicked curled on my lips as I pulled into a parking spot. He was just as excited as I was, even if he didn't want to admit it.

His lips quirked into a similar smile as he made a show of looking at his watch before sauntering over to the passenger side. Finn hopped into the backseat before I even asked and wagged her tail as Paul got in.

"Looks like someone got antsy."

"Hey, I'm not the one standing outside in the heat."

I grinned and elbowed him in the side as he put his seatbelt on. His nose was a little red, and he looked tired.

"Geez, how late were you up?" I asked as I turned around to back out of the spot.

"Four. I was too jacked up after getting the print run done to go to sleep. You know how it is. You'd think after doing this twice a week for two years I'd get over it."

Paul's first love was news, which was probably the reason his marriage to Christine, his high school sweetheart, hadn't worked out. They'd split amicably, and the last I'd heard, she was remarried and had a kid, but for Paul, the news was his baby. He poured his heart and soul into the newspaper.

"What are you going to do when you take it daily? You can't just live like a vampire. You need to hire some help, Paul."

"I know. It's tough finding the right person, though. I want to compete with the big papers in Denver. I've got a job listing posted. We'll just have to see. But yeah, I'm putting off my plans until I can find someone."

I nodded and pulled out of the parking lot, heading for the highway. I glanced at Paul as he turned and ruffled the fur on Finn's head and nodded at Briar.

"You'll figure it out, Paul. You always do. I wish there was something I could do to help, but I'm pretty sure you got all the creative genes in the family."

He turned back around and shrugged before pulling his phone out of his pocket.

"You'll want to turn left up here. I appreciate it, Tess. I wouldn't have made it this far without your support."

I rolled my eyes but turned left, following his directions.

"Okay, so I guess you're my navigator today, huh?"

He grinned and leaned his head back on the headrest before reaching for the radio dial.

"Well, I don't feel like getting lost. What are we listening to? What sandwiches did you bring?"

I smacked his hand away, narrowing my eyes.

"Good music. Driver gets to pick. You know the rules."

"Well, when the driver has terrible taste in music, those rules are void. Brother sister agreement page twenty-five, paragraph four. The oldest always gets to pick the music."

I made a raspberry sound and smacked his hand away again.

"Leave it. I like this song. So, did you remember our great aunt? Since you're so much wiser, you know. And older. I brought peanut butter and jelly sandwiches. They're behind your seat if you want to grab them."

"I'm not that old. And no. I can honestly say I've never seen or heard of this woman. I'm still pretty sure it's a mistake. I tried calling the attorney's office, but nobody answered. I have a feeling this is just an enormous waste of time."

He handed me an unwrapped sandwich before biting into his.

"Hey, you never know. I'm still hoping we'll walk away as newly minted millionaires. You'd be able to hire an entire staff and live the high life."

Paul snorted and looked out the window, his eyebrows pulled down in a frown. I took a bite of my sandwich and smiled around the peanut butter. You couldn't beat a classic.

"I think I'd get bored. But what about you? What would you do if you came into money?"

I opened my mouth and then closed it. What would I do? We'd been solidly middle-class my entire life. Not uncomfortable, but definitely not well-off. Our parents had taught us that if we wanted something, we saved until we had the money to buy it outright. As a teenager, that had rankled to no end, but now, as an adult rapidly approaching thirty-two, I saw the sense in it.

"I honestly don't know," I said, finally. "I wouldn't know what to do with that kind of money. I'd probably start an animal sanctuary or something."

Paul snorted and shook his head.

"My sister, the cat lady."

"Hey, I don't see you back on the dating market. It's been years since you and Christine split up. You're a decent-looking guy, even if you are my brother. You deserve to find some happiness."

Paul mock-glared at me before rolling his eyes.

"I will. I'm busy, though. I have little time for dating."

"Meggie's single again. You know…"

His brown eyes met mine as I glanced away from the road. For once, they were serious.

"Tessa, I will not date your best friend. That would just be weird. What if things didn't work out? How awkward would that be?"

I looked away, uncertain. Meggie had carried a torch for my brother from the first time we met, back in the third grade. She'd never act on it, having said something very similar to what Paul just said. Instead, she dated a string of men I knew she wasn't really interested in. I heaved a sigh and shook my head.

"But what if they did? Work out, I mean. What if?"

"Not a risk I'm willing to take, kiddo. Turn right up here, we're almost there."

And that was the end of that conversation. I filed it away, determined to return to it at a later date. A much later date. But I'd never let it go, not completely. Somehow, I knew if they'd just take the leap, they'd find out they were perfect for each other.

"What's the name of that lawyer again?" I asked, steering towards safer ground.

"Endicoot?"

"I think it was Endicott, but thanks for that. Now I'm probably going to call him that to his face, and it will be all I can think of when I look at him."

Paul snickered and shifted in his seat as we passed a sign welcoming us to Welder, Colorado, population, two-hundred-and-fifteen. He let out a whistle.

"A bustling community. Where do they put them all?"

He raised a good point. From what I could see, the town of Welder comprised the main road, full of rickety looking buildings that appeared as though they'd fall down if a stiff wind blew, and a few other side streets. Given how close we were to the Wyoming border, notorious for its windy conditions, I couldn't believe the town still stood.

"I don't know. Maybe the sign is out of date. Do you think that's the building?"

I pointed towards the brown, squatty building next to the post office. A large sign with faded paint said LAW.

"You missed your calling as a detective, Tess."

I thwacked him across the arm as I slowed down and pulled into a parking spot. There were plenty to pick from, as the entire town appeared to be deserted. A shiver went down my spine.

"Uh, this feels weird. Why is there no one around? I mean, I get that it's midday on a Wednesday, but this place looks deserted."

Paul made an eerie woo-woo noise, and I rolled my eyes.

"I'm being serious. What if we're about to be killed by an axe-murderer? This place is giving 'the hills have eyes vibes' left and right."

"Only one way to find out. I'm sure it's one of those towns where everyone works someplace else and just comes here to sleep. It's probably bustling on the weekends. Let's check it out. We're early, but the letter just said to be here before two."

He hopped out and shut the door, staring up and down the street. Finn leapt into his vacated seat and let out a low whine. I rubbed her head and nodded.

"Exactly. I don't know about this girl. What do you think?"

Finn stared at the building and gave me a look that said I was crazy if I was thinking about going in there, but Paul was already walking up to the door. I couldn't let my brother go into a murder nest alone. I sighed and cranked the AC.

"We'll be back. I hope."

I slid out of the car, catching Briar's eye as I closed my door. I smiled and trotted to catch up with Paul.

"Hang on, I'm coming."

He put his hand on the door handle and tried it. Surprisingly, it swung open. He held it for me and motioned with his arm.

"After you."

Great, my brother, the gentleman. Sending me into the murder nest first. I resisted the urge to stick out my tongue at him and walked inside. The air smelled musty, but it was much cooler that the sidewalk. I looked around the interior and glanced back at Paul.

It was as though we'd stepped back in time. The furniture, crowded into the small entry area, was ancient. Paul let out a low whistle, his fingers twitching.

"That's gotta be mahogany. Look at that shine. That desk would sell for five thousand these days."

"Shh. Where is everyone? Shouldn't there be a receptionist?"

"Mr. Endicott?"

I winced, grateful he hadn't said Endicoot, but his voice sounded overly loud in the hushed confines of the office building. It felt almost like a church, a place where loud noises were banned, and miscreants would be punished. A shiver worked its way down my spine.

"I think we should go. There's no one here. This is just strange."

As I spoke, a door at the back of the room swung open revealing a tall, cadaverous man, with a lean face and eyes that shone, even in the dim light coming through the frosted windows. His charcoal gray suit looked almost as ancient as he did, but it was nicely tailored and obviously expensive. No hair graced his shiny scalp.

"You must be the Windsors. Please, come back."

He stepped back into the hallway and I turned to look at Paul, my eyes flaring wide. This did not seem like a good idea. Nope. Not at all. Paul shrugged and headed for the hall, leaving me behind. I could stand there by myself, or follow my brother into the unknown. I heaved another sigh and scurried to catch up. I did not know what we were getting ourselves into.

Chapter Three

Reginald Endicott's office was as dank and dismal as the front entrance, and, if possible, was stuffed with even more antiques. I wasn't much for fancy furniture, preferring my pieces to be as cheap as possible, if not free, but even I couldn't believe the bookcase that towered behind the man's desk. It, like everything else in the room, was made with mahogany wood, and the surface gleamed with a luster at odds with the general air of disrepair of the rest of the place.

There were two leather chairs facing the giant desk, and Paul and I sank down next to one another. The surface of the chair was slightly cold, and I regretted wearing my choice of my usual attire of cargo shorts until the leather warmed to my skin. I'd regret that choice again. Later, when I stood up, I just knew it.

"I trust you both received your letters from my courier this morning?"

Endicott's voice creaked like a rickety step. Like perhaps he didn't speak often. I glanced at Paul before nodding.

"Yes. But we don't understand. As far as we know, we don't have a great aunt named Euphemia. I'm sure there's been some sort of mistake. We tried to call..."

He held up a bony hand, cutting me off, and frowned.

"I assure you I do not make mistakes. Miss Hawthorne entrusted me to carry out her last wishes, and that was to find her remaining relatives."

Paul cleared his throat and straightened in his chair, making the leather creak.

"How are we related to Miss Hawthorne? I'm sorry, it's just that we've never heard of her before."

"She is your great aunt on your father's side. As you know, your father was an only child, and he is the son of an only child. Miss Hawthorne never married."

"She's from this town? I can't believe we grew up just forty-five minutes from here and never heard of her. I'm sorry, it's not that we're ungrateful," I said, as he frowned at me, his thin eyebrows slanting towards his nose. "It's just so very unexpected."

"Miss Hawthorne has left both of you a bequest and very specific instructions," he said, ignoring my question. "Now that you are here, we can proceed."

"I'm sorry," I said, flushing a little. "But your letter said that if we didn't show up today, our inheritance would be forfeit. Since we're her only two living relatives, who would it go to?"

"Failure was not an option, but in the unlikely event that you chose not to come, the bequest was to be destroyed."

He pulled out a silver pocket watch and frowned again, his brows making an arrow shape that led right to his dissatisfied expression. He stowed the watch away and turned to the bookcase behind him. As he swiveled back, his hands held a small, carved wooden box.

"Time grows short. Miss Hawthorne requested I give you this box. It is to be opened here, immediately. If you choose to leave the box closed, you will lose the contents. You are to be left alone to make your decision. I will give you fifteen minutes. Once the box has been opened, there is no turning back. If you will excuse me, I will leave you to your deliberations."

He put the box on the desk in front of us and left, closing the door behind him with a snick that seemed to echo through the room. I tore my eyes away from the box long enough to look at my brother.

"So, um, this is odd, right?"

"It's beautiful. Look at this pattern, Tess," Paul said, reaching tentative hands towards the box.

I scooted forward, my hands automatically reaching for him. Somehow, I didn't want him to touch that box. I didn't know why, but I had a feeling that once we opened it, our lives were going to change. That everything was going to change.

I was too slow. His hand stroked the wooden carvings, and he squinted as he held the box closer.

"Look at this, Tess. It's got a tiny cat with a dog next to it, carved on the top. They look just like Finn and Briar. And over here, on the sides, those are newspapers."

My mouth went dry as I leaned closer to see the carvings. He was right. The animals bore a striking resemblance to my pets, even down to the long-haired cat. I swallowed hard, desperate for some moisture in my mouth.

"I don't know about this, Paul. I don't think we should open it. This is just too strange. I mean, that Endicott guy... he's super different. This whole thing is odd. The courier, the letters, the great aunt we've never heard of until this morning."

Paul's eyes never left the box, but he shook his head.

"We have to open it. We've come all this way. We can't stop now. I mean, we're here. Aren't you just a little curious about what's inside?"

I shifted in my seat, the leather sticking unpleasantly to my thighs. Yep, I was right, Regrets aplenty.

"I mean, yeah. A little. But what if it's something bad? Something, I don't know, evil? You know those movies where you want to scream at the people on the screen not to open the darn box? That's us, Paul. We're about to do something we can never take back. We're like that Pandora chick."

"I don't think we're going to end paradise on earth by opening it, though. It's not like you to be this dramatic," Paul said, finally looking at me. "You're serious, aren't you?"

I nodded and chewed on my lip.

"I just... I don't know. This all feels super bizarre. I mean, we've got fifteen minutes to decide, right? What's the rush? Let's think about this."

A small smile curved on Paul's lips and he sat back.

"Alright. So, the box is small. I'd say it's about eight inches by four. Obviously, it doesn't contain a million bucks."

"Unless there's a check inside. That would fit in there."

"True. Something tells me, though, that good old Aunt Euphemia didn't have a million bucks. Especially if she lived in this town. Besides, in your story, she papered her walls with it, right?"

"I was thinking more of her using it as insulation, but yeah. Okay, so it's not money. Unless it's a check. Which isn't likely. What else could fit inside of there?"

"There's only one way to find out, Tess. Let's do it."

Trepidation crept up my spine on spidery feet as Paul reached for the box again, but I said nothing. He was right. We could talk about it until we were out of time and we'd never know for sure until we opened it. I took a deep breath and nodded.

"Do it."

He lifted the lid, and we peered into the box, so close to each other that my ponytail brushed his cheek. A bright light shot out and hovered over it. I gasped, eyes wide.

"Look! It's a tiny dragonfly. Or a lightning bug. How is it glowing like that?"

Whatever it was, it zipped around the two of us for a moment before hovering again, right between us. It was almost as if it was deciding. With a strange trilling noise, it shot into the air right above me and darted down, landing on my hand.

I blinked as I gently lifted my hand to get a closer look at the creature. I had to squint as the light flared. Tickling feet stroked my hand, and the light grew so bright I cried out as I shut my eyes. When I opened them again, it was gone.

My mouth fell open, and I looked at Paul. He was ashen.

"What? Where did it go?"

"Um. Inside you. When you cried out, the light or the bug, or whatever it was, it jumped in your mouth."

I jumped up, not even caring that the leather chair peeled off part of my skin and danced around in place, pawing at my face.

"Gross! Get it out, get it out!"

Paul put a hand on my arm and stood.

"Open your mouth."

I closed my eyes and opened my mouth as he leaned closer. It was taking too long, and I risked opening an eye.

"It is still in there?"

"Uh. No. Nothing but your teeth and a few fillings. Well, that was weird."

"Weird? I just had some strange light bug thing fly into my mouth and the best word you can come up with is weird? You're the writer, for crying out loud. Oh gosh, what if it makes me sick? I felt nothing in my mouth. I don't remember swallowing. Where did it go? Am I going to get sick? Am I going to die? Oh gosh, what would happen to Finn and Briar if I did? Paul!"

He sat back down heavily and stared at the box.

"It's like it disappeared and the light shot into you. But it was just light. I don't think it could actually hurt you. You look fine. Maybe it was all just an illusion. That makes the most sense. It was a trick of the light or something. What else do you think is in there?"

"I don't know and I don't want to," I said, backing away from the desk. "I'm pretty sure this is all just a strange dream and I'm going to wake up in my cabin. That's it. I had jalapeños on my pizza last night. Maybe that did it."

He huffed a laugh and shook his head.

"Sorry, Tess. I'm pretty sure we're awake. Look, there's something else in the box."

"Nope. Not looking. I'm going to wake up. Any minute now, I'm going to wake up. Don't do it, Paul."

He reached in and I bit back a gasp as he pulled out a key. It was tiny and looked old. Ancient. He turned it around in his fingers.

"It looks like a safe deposit box key. You remember when mom and dad had one? It looked just like this. I wonder which bank it's from."

A knock rapped on the door and I almost jumped out of my skin as the door swung open and Reginald Endicott Esquire came back into the room. He saw the open box and the key in Paul's hand and nodded slowly.

"Very good. Miss Hawthorne would be thrilled to know that the bequest had been accepted. The key, Mr. Windsor, belongs to the First National Bank in Collinsville. You are to present yourself there by tomorrow, with identification. The contents of the safe deposit box are yours. The other item was intended for Miss Windsor, if she was worthy."

"Um, what? Worthy? Of having a lightning bug or whatever it was, zip into my mouth? What is going on here? Nothing makes sense."

He pulled the pocket watch out again and ignored me.

"If you'll excuse me, I must be going. The box is yours to take, Miss Windsor. The key belongs to you, Paul."

He stood and pointed towards the door, waiting for us to leave. I shook my head as my emotions tripped over themselves as they tried to decide which one was going to come out first. Anger won.

"Excuse me, but you can't just toss us out of your office. We have questions. What is going on?"

"I'm afraid I cannot answer those questions. I was hired to discharge a duty, and that duty has been done. If you'll excuse my supposition, I believe the rest of your questions might be answered when you retrieve the rest of your bequest in the safe deposit box. Now, if you'll excuse me, I am a very busy man."

Paul gathered up the box, took my arm, and steered me out of the office while I spluttered. Endicott followed us like the grim reaper, making sure we vacated the premises as quickly as possible. Once we were on the sidewalk, the door slammed shut and I heard the lock turn.

"Wait a minute," I said, turning back and knocking on the door. "Please, Mr. Endicott, we need more information. You can't just kick us out."

"Uh, Tess. That's what he did. Come on, let's get out of here. If we hurry, we can get to the bank before it closes. Maybe we'll get some answers there."

I was steaming mad, but after knocking two more times, with no result, I knew he was right. Endicott, even if he had our answers, wasn't talking.

"Fine. But this is too much."

"I'll drive," Paul said, darting around to the driver's side.

"Hey!"

It was too late. He was already inside, grinning at me. I rolled my eyes and stomped over to the passenger side. Today was not going anything like I thought it would, and I wasn't waking up. This wasn't a dream, but that didn't mean I understood what was going on. My hand went to my mouth after I climbed in, and I couldn't help but wonder what happened to the little bug. I swallowed hard and tried not to envision it flying around inside my stomach as we headed back to Collinsville. Could this day get any stranger?

Chapter Four

The empty town of Welder wasn't any less spooky as I sat and fastened my seat belt. In fact, it felt even weirder than it had when we'd first arrived. No one was around and I half expected to see a lone tumbleweed cruising down the street. Paul handed me the box as he pulled out of the parking spot and I took it gingerly, glancing back at my pets.

"You're sure you got everything out of this? No more nasty surprises?"

Finn pressed her cold nose into the back of my arm, making me jump. She wagged her plumed, white-tipped tail, and gave me a doggy smile before woofing softly.

"See, she's telling you not to worry. Whatever happened in there, well, I don't know what to say. I think it was all an illusion. That guy probably had a projector or something hidden away in his office, and it made us think there was a magical lightning bug. It wasn't real. I mean, it's a downer to open a box that looks that cool, and the only thing inside is a tiny key."

"A projection? Yeah, maybe," I said, tracing the carved pattern on the box. "But why does this box have a dog and a cat on it? And a newspaper? That's a little too coincidental, isn't it? I mean, come on, Paul. What are the odds?"

He shrugged and tossed me an exasperated glance as we headed down the highway, back to Collinsville.

"I don't know, Tess. Maybe we'll get our answers at the bank. This is all just really weird. How did this lady know so much about us and we've never met her? Something isn't adding up."

"I'm gonna ask mom. She's got to know. Or if she doesn't, she's the only one who can get the story out of dad. You know what he's like."

Paul and I both took after our mother, both in looks and temperament. Our dad was the strong, silent type. I'd never seen him cry once. In fact, if I did, it would be so earth-shattering, I wouldn't know what to do. He said little, but one thing was certain: we always knew we were loved.

"I'll let you handle that," Paul said, grimacing. "You know how much mom loves to talk. The last time she called me, I think I was on the phone for three hours."

"She loves you, Paul. And it's because you never call her, so she's got to talk longer."

He shrugged again and turned on the radio, smirking at me as he changed the channel to classic rock. I rolled my eyes, but said nothing as I stared out the window. He was obviously done talking about it, even though I had plenty of questions I needed to ask. I looked down at the box on my lap, still intrigued by the pattern on it. A soft voice behind me sounded. Somehow, it was almost familiar, even though at that moment, I'd swear I'd never heard it before.

"What do you think happened in there? She's worried. I can feel it. I don't like it. She feels all squiggly on the inside."

I blinked and looked at Paul, and then at the dash, staring at the radio. A song was playing, the singer crooning about how the boys were back in town. The singer was male. Not a woman.

"It's something to do with that box she's holding. I need to get up there and get a sniff. I agree, she's not acting like herself. I don't like it either."

I looked down at the box again, my heart pounding. What was I hearing? This voice was distinct, throatier somehow. Almost scratchy. I reached a hand for the dial and Paul shook his head.

"Nope. He who drives picks the tunes."

"Shhh."

I turned off the dial and waited, feeling more than a little silly as Paul raised an eyebrow, and turned to look at me.

"Did you just shush me?"

"Shhh!!"

"I'll distract her and you get up there in her lap. I'm too big. I might break the box. We've got to see what's bothering her."

I blinked several times and slowly pivoted in my seat, staring at Finn and Briar. Their heads were together.

"Tess? Tessa? What's wrong? Why are you acting so weird?"

I held up a hand, cutting off Paul, and licked my lips. This was bonkers. I had to be imagining it. Right? Cats and dogs didn't talk. Not in real life. I went out on a limb, a very shaky one, and spoke, my voice cracking.

"Uh, hi guys. If you want to see the box, you can just ask me."

Finn and Briar slowly turned towards me, their eyes flaring so wide it would've been comical if the situation had been different. If the situation hadn't been the fact that they obviously understood me and I'd really overheard them. Holy smokes, was I losing my mind?

"Oh..."

That was Briar. Her mouth moved. I saw it. She glanced at Finn, who was goggling at me as though I had not one, but potentially three heads. She gulped as our eyes locked.

"Uh... you can hear us?"

That sweet voice belonged to Finn. My beautiful border collie, who I had since she was a pup, was speaking. And I understood every single word. I nearly passed out.

"Tessa, you've gone white as a sheet. What's wrong? Who are you talking to? The dog and cat?"

I nodded and grabbed onto his arm, squeezing so hard he yelped.

"Paul, I can hear them. They're speaking. In English. And I understand them."

I jerked forward, my seat belt tightening painfully on my shoulder, as Paul slammed on the brakes in the middle of the highway, jostling Finn and Briar in the backseat. Luckily, we were the only ones on the road, or that could have ended really badly.

"Paul! What are you doing?"

He let off the brakes and coasted over to the side of the road where he deliberately put my Land Rover in park and looked at me, his pale face pulled into an expression of concern.

"Do you have a fever? How many fingers am I holding up? You didn't hit your head, did you?"

I shifted in my seat, rubbing at my neck, and shook my head before flipping him off.

"You're holding up three fingers. How many am I holding up? You could have gotten us all killed. I can't believe you just did that. Guys, are you okay?"

I looked in the backseat as Finn nodded, her expression sheepish.

"Yes, but one of my nails went through the seat. I'm so sorry. You can understand us? Truly?"

I felt as though I was in another dimension as I nodded slowly.

"I can. Paul, can you pinch me? I want to make sure I'm not dreaming. Can you hear them, too? Ouch! Not that hard."

"Hey, you told me to pinch you. I can hear Briar meowing, and Finn is woofing like she always does, but are you saying you are hearing them speak? Like sentences?"

Briar turned towards my brother, her green eyes narrowing.

"Yes, in complete, grammatically correct sentences. Which is more than I can say for you."

I bit my lip, but the laugh I was attempting to hold back escaped. My shoulders shook as Paul turned towards me, his eyes narrowing too.

"What did she just say?"

I repeated it word for word, while Briar watched me, her eyes lit with fascination. I shook my head and reached for her, stroking her soft fur.

"I can't believe it. It had to be the light, right Paul? The bug, or whatever it was? It gave me some sort of magical power."

"Or maybe you're right and we really are in a dream. Tess, I love you to bits, but pets can't talk. I know you talk to them all the time, but they can't answer you. This isn't happening. It's not real."

Briar leapt over the console, landing lightly on my lap, and began sniffing the wooden box, her sides going in and out. She sat and stared up at me, eyes wide.

"I don't think you're far off on the magical power thing. This box positively reeks of magic. Tell me what happened. From start to finish."

I glanced at Paul before laying out our visit inside Endicott's office. Once I was done, she looked at Finn and nodded.

"That's why she felt. What word did you use? Squiggly? The magic is meshing into her blood."

"I see," Finn said. "Will she be alright?"

"Yes. Once the meshing is complete, she'll be fine."

I swallowed hard and couldn't hold back a shudder. Meshing?

"Is there anything I can do? And just how do you know so much about magic, Briar?" I asked, tilting my head to the side.

"What?" Paul asked, his question exploding between us. "Magic? Now you've really gone off the deep end. Pets can't talk, Tessa. This is just too bizarre."

Briar pivoted, one of her sharp claws digging into my thigh, and fastened a look on my brother. I eased out her claw, wincing at the scratch she'd left behind.

"Tell him I know he was the one who ruined your favorite kitchen towel. The one you crocheted. It happened five weeks ago when he visited the cabin. He wasn't paying attention, and it was in the sink when he turned on the disposal. It was shredded, and he hid the evidence in the garbage can."

It was my turn to goggle at the cat in my lap before turning an accusatory stare towards my brother.

"What? I've looked everywhere for that towel."

"Tell him. Word for word."

I repeated her words and watched as my brother stared at Briar like he'd seen a ghost. Or, at the very least, a talking cat. Which apparently Briar was. He paled even further and whispered.

"How? How is this possible?"

"So, she's right?"

"Of course I'm right. I was sitting on the countertop when it happened. You were outside with Finn, playing fetch."

"Oh, that was a very nice game of fetch," Finn said. "I remember that."

"And it's not like you're the only one who can talk to us. Eden and Hannah could. You could've knocked me over with a feather when Eden spoke to me for the first time. Finn and I have been wishing for something like this to happen. And it finally did!"

My mouth dropped open as I looked down at my cat. Eden Brooks and Hannah Murphy had been on one of my hikes a few weeks ago. It had been an unmitigated disaster, but they'd quickly become friends of mine. Now I was just finding out they could talk to my animals? Before I even could?

Finn nuzzled my hand.

"They couldn't talk to me, though. Just Briar. They were nice. We both liked them a lot. Razzy and Gus were amazing cats. So polite."

Briar's eyes held a fond gleam as she looked into the backseat before turning her focus on me. Paul sat, gaping like a fish, while Briar spoke again.

"You never possessed magic before. You had the capability, but no spark. Now? You've got the spark."

Her words settled into my heart, and it was like something clicked and came together. I didn't know how this happened. I didn't know why. But I knew I'd just been given an incredible gift. Peace and acceptance filled my soul, and I wrapped her in a hug, like I always did, but my hands slowed as I realized she had her own autonomy. She was a thinking, feeling, talking creature. I cleared my throat.

"May I hug you?"

She inclined her head and her green eyes twinkled.

"Of course, silly goose. Just because you can understand us now means nothing has to change. You're still you. And we're still, well, us. And in a way, we've always been able to communicate. I'll say, for a human, you're a pretty good one."

I had the feeling that was high praise, considering what I knew of Briar. When I'd adopted the two of them as a package deal from the shelter, the staff had known little of the cat, just that she'd appeared one day, right before Finn arrived. She'd moved into Finn's cage, refusing to leave, and they'd been inseparable. I gently folded her into a hug and pressed a kiss on the top of her forehead.

A lick on my cheek startled me and I turned to see Finn's beautiful dark eyes looking into mine, her nose so close I could see down it.

"This is the best day ever," she said, eyes shining. "I can't believe it."

Paul cleared his throat as I pressed a kiss on Finn's head and I turned to look at him. He was still frightfully pale and looked like he was going to be sick.

"If we're going to make it to the bank in time, we'd better hurry," I said, glancing at the clock on the dash. "Whatever that key opens belongs to you. Remember what Endicott said?"

Paul nodded stiffly, and we pulled off the side of the road, merging back onto the highway. His voice was so quiet I almost missed what he said.

"What if I don't want it?"

My stomach lurched as I reached across to him. I still didn't know what was going on, but the wonder I felt surpassed any trepidation. If this was a dream, it was a darn good one. If it wasn't, I knew my life had just changed amazingly. I patted his arm and smiled.

"You'll make that decision when it comes, and I'll support you. No matter what. Like I always have."

He gave me a shaky smile, and we continued towards Collinsville, each of us wrapped in our thoughts. Briar curled in my lap, her soft purr lulling me into a contented daze. I didn't know why the magic had chosen me, or whatever happened in Endicott's office, but I was glad it had. So very glad.

Chapter Five

By the time we'd pulled into the parking lot at the bank, we had just fifteen minutes left before it closed. Paul and I had said little on the rest of the drive, but he seemed at ease, calmer, than he had twenty minutes ago. I patted Briar and turned to put her in the backseat, next to Finn.

"We'll be right back, okay? We've got to go see what this key will unlock."

"Hey, if you're a witch, maybe I'll get to be a wizard," Paul said, brightening. "Or would that be a warlock?"

"You always loved fantasy books, didn't you? I remember when you were in middle school, you locked yourself away for weeks while you read the *Lord of the Rings*. You were obsessed."

"Still am, if I'm being honest. How cool would that be, though?"

"Pretty outstanding. Well, let's see what's waiting for you in the vault. Now, that sounded creepy, didn't it?"

"You shall not pass," Paul said with a wink. "I'll leave the AC on for these guys."

A thought occurred to me as I looked at my pets in the backseat.

For as long as they'd known me, I'd tried to make sure they were well fed, loved, and cared for, but I'd never known their likes and dislikes.

"What kind of music do you like? I can leave the radio on for you."

Briar shuddered delicately.

"Anything but that channel Paul picked. Finn's not a fan of country music, either. Personally, I prefer classical."

"I like that, too. Or maybe some pop music. Anything with a good beat," Finn said, her voice filled with laughter.

I grinned, unable to help myself, and switched it to the local pop station.

"We'll be back soon."

I closed the door and joined Paul on the other side of the vehicle. He looked shell-shocked, but at least he wasn't as pale as he'd been before. I elbowed him lightly in the side as we crossed the parking lot.

"You're taking this really well," Paul said, shading his eyes from the sun as he looked at me.

"Are you kidding me? It's been my dream to talk to animals since I was a little girl. You remember when I went through my Snow White phase?"

He snorted as he held the door open for me and we walked into the lobby.

"How could I forget? I'm still deaf in one ear from the caterwauling you called singing. You insisted on walking through the forest every single day, convinced that birds and squirrels would flock to you."

I narrowed my eyes, but I couldn't fling back a scathing comment since we were standing in front of the woman behind the customer service counter. I kept up the glare, but he smiled before turning towards the woman. Was it my imagination, or did she just melt a little as he turned the full force of his smile on her? No, I wasn't imagining it. Paul was my brother, but I knew full well the effect he had on women.

"Good afternoon," he said, glancing at the nameplate on the

desk. "Shelby. We're here to get into a safe deposit box. I've got the key, but I'm uncertain which number it is. This is all I have."

He passed over the black key and the woman's sunny expression dimmed a bit. Her ivory forehead furrowed as she looked between us.

"This is from our old vault. If you don't have a number, I'll need your names and I'll need to see some identification."

I pawed through my bag, searching for my wallet, while Paul slid his ID across the counter. She took it with a smile as their fingers brushed and I rolled my eyes as I finally found my wallet at the very bottom of my bag. I pried my ID out and handed it over. I didn't get the same big smile, but at least she gave me a friendly nod.

"It's been years since I've seen one of those keys," she said, as she looked at her computer screen. "You're lucky that we digitized everything. Before, we'd have to go through this giant ledger to find names. There you are, Paul Windsor. And Tessa. Married?"

"She's my sister," Paul said, grinning as he took his ID back.

Preserve me from witnessing my brother flirting with a woman. I folded my arms over my chest and looked around the lobby. I hadn't been to this bank before, but I knew it was one of the oldest banks in the area. The original bank had been torn down back in the sixties and rebuilt in the same spot.

"If you'll follow me, we'll go down to the old vault," Shelby said, clipping an ID card to her jacket's lapel.

I hung back, giving them space to do whatever it was they were doing, and looked around with interest as we got deeper into the bank. We passed through a room lined with small boxes, and then Shelby came to a stop in front of an ornately arched door. She scanned the card on her lapel and the door slid open.

"We upgraded the tech around the vault, but preserved the original structure. It's really something."

She wasn't kidding. The room we were standing in looked old and smelled far older. The intricately carved crown molding soared over heads, and Shelby's heels sounded like hammers as she walked across the marble floor.

"Box number seventy-seven is yours. I'll leave you two to go through the contents while I wait outside. If you need anything, or when you're ready to leave, just push the red button right there next to the door."

She nodded, tossing my brother a warm smile, before scanning her card and disappearing through the sliding door. I shoved my hands in my pockets and nodded at Paul.

"Alright. Here we are. Let's do this."

He chewed on his lips before nodding and turning to the bank of tiny drawers behind us. It didn't take him long to find the one we were looking for. One turn with the black key and a long, thin drawer slid free.

He carried it back to the low table in the center of the room and looked at me.

"Ready for this?"

"As I'm going to be. But if there's another one of those lightning bugs, I'm diving under the table. You get the next one, okay? I've had enough strange stuff today."

He smirked and inserted the key into the lock on the box. A shivery sound echoed through the room as he lifted the lid. I peeked over his shoulder and blinked. Honestly, I didn't know what to expect, but what was at the bottom of the box was disappointing. All it held was a small, pocket-sized book and an envelope that had seen a better day.

Paul raised an eyebrow, and I shrugged.

"Open it. It belongs to you."

"Am I kind of weird for hoping it's a treasure map? How cool would that be?" Paul said as he gingerly picked up the envelope by the corner.

The paper might have been white at one point, but now it was yellowed and it looked brittle. Like if one of us breathed too hard on it, the paper would flake into a million pieces. I held my breath as Paul eased open the flap. Two sheets of paper were inside. He carefully unfolded it. The sheet on top was covered in spidery writing. My brother let out a reverent breath as he smoothed the surface.

"It's a letter. And it's addressed to you," I said, wincing at how loud my voice sounded in the vault.

It might have been my imagination, but Paul's hands seemed to tremble as he began reading.

"Dear Paul, I'm certain this has all come as a surprise to you and your sister. If I know your father, he's never mentioned me. While I was alive, I followed his request to never contact you, but now that I am dead, the bargain has ended. Even though you weren't aware of me, I've paid close attention to the two of you throughout your lives. You are the last of my line, you see, and I wanted to make certain you were ready."

"Ready? For what?" I said, leaning over his shoulder as he read. "What does she mean? The last of what line?"

"If you'd let me continue, I'm sure we'll find out," Paul said, his tone dry. "She was watching us? That's not creepy or anything."

"Right? Why wouldn't he let us know about her? I don't understand."

He shrugged and picked up where he left off.

"Your sister has been chosen as a vessel of the magic I carried my entire life. I received it from my grandmother at her passing. Do not feel left out, Paul. This power must always go to the women in our family. If it deemed your sister worthy, it will be her responsibility to pass it along to the next generation. But that doesn't mean you're left with nothing. In this box, you will find two things. A deed to a property and a special book. It's always been fickle, so be careful with it. I wish you both luck. You'll need it. All my love and light, your great aunt, Euphemia."

We both let out a breath and stared at each other, and then looked down into the box. The book looked unremarkable. Small, rather dingy, and worn.

"Guess it found you worthy, Tess," he said, finally. "A special book? I wonder what it can do?"

He picked it up and turned it over in his hand. There was no writing on either side, but it was quite thick. Paul moved to open the book, but nothing happened.

"Huh. The pages must be fused together. It looks super old. I don't want to tear it," he said, as he turned it over again.

"What about the deed? What kind of property is it? Oh, I hope it's not a house in Welder. That town was creepy."

He passed the letter over to me and I trailed my fingers over it, wishing I could have known the woman who wrote it. I had reams of questions and no one to answer them. What kind of magic had I inherited? Was it even possible? I mean, obviously, I could hear my pets, but what other things could I do?

"It's got the survey coordinates, but no address," Paul said, as he scanned the other paper in his hand. "It's too late now to go to the courthouse, but it looks like it's here in Collinsville. This is so weird."

I nodded as I passed the letter back to him.

"I think we need to call our parents. They've got some explaining to do."

He snorted and looked at the book again.

"No kidding. Well, I guess we've got what we came for. Let's get out of here."

My heart clenched at the look on his face. It felt like Paul had gotten the short end of the stick. A book that wouldn't open and a deed to something. I brightened as he folded up the letter and the deed.

"Hey, maybe it's a mansion! You can finally move out of that tiny apartment. How nice would that be?"

"Unless it's a money pit," he snorted as he tucked the book into his back pocket. "That deed is old. I think they've gone to an entirely new system since this was created."

"Well, I guess we'll find out tomorrow. And maybe that book is super cool and rare. What do you think she meant by it being fickle? How can a book be fickle?"

Paul's eyes gleamed as he slid the box back into its slot in the wall and locked the door.

"Maybe it's magic, too. I'll see if I can get it open later. Push the button. I suppose we can close the box, since we've got everything we needed."

I glanced at the wall where the box was safely tucked away and shrugged before tapping the button next to the door. It whooshed open, and we headed out.

"I guess you're right. I just can't believe we never knew her. I wonder if she was lonely. No family around to take care of her. It's sad."

He nodded as Shelby pushed off the wall where she was leaning and smiled at us.

"All set?"

Paul nodded and handed the key over to her.

"Yep. We can close the box. It's empty now."

She took the key and nodded before leading us back through the newer vault towards the main lobby of the bank.

"I'll take care of that. If you want to open an account with us, just let me know. Here, let me give you my card. It's got my cellphone on it if you need anything after hours."

Paul took it with a smile and I wondered briefly if he picked up on the undertones. Knowing him, he probably missed it. He'd missed Meggie's undying devotion to him for the past twelve years.

"Thanks, Shelby."

We walked back out into the oppressive heat, and I jogged around to the driver's side and held out my hand.

"My turn to drive. I know we did little today, but I'm exhausted. I can't wait to get home, eat some supper and go to bed."

He tossed me the keys, and I hopped in, smiling at Finn as she leapt over the console to go back to the backseat.

"Thanks, girl."

"I enjoy looking out. The view back here isn't as nice," she said, dipping her head shyly.

"Good to know. I bet you guys are hungry, huh?"

Briar sounded a little grumpy when she answered.

"Starved. That took long enough. What did you find in there?"

I grinned like a loon as I pulled out of our parking spot. I certainly hadn't expected to be interrogated by a cat today, but something about it felt right. I filled her in as we drove back to Paul's apartment. She put a paw on Paul's arm and he jumped, looking down at it.

"The book. Please, may I see it?"

I translated for him and he shifted in his seat, so he could get it out of his pocket. He held it for the cat as she sniffed it thoroughly. I turned the corner and cruised into the parking lot at Paul's place, finding a spot near the door. I left the engine running and Briar finished her perusal.

"Finn, what do you think?" Briar asked, looking over her shoulder.

The border collie leaned forward, eyes bright, as she sniffed the cover, being careful not to touch it.

"Oh, this is special," she said, glancing at me. "It has the same squiggly feel as you did when you got in the car back there."

"Agreed," Briar said, nodding as she looked up at Paul, green eyes wide. "Be careful with this. Very careful."

Paul waited, not so patiently, as they spoke. I repeated what they said while eyeing the book nervously.

"Interesting," he said, looking down at the book with awe. "I've always wished for something like this. I hope I can open it."

Briar looked like she was going to speak, but shook her head slightly and went back to her spot next to Finn.

I frowned and glanced at Paul.

"Be careful, okay? Maybe don't open it when you're alone?"

He shrugged and grinned as he slid out of his seat.

"Yeah, not happening. See you later, Tess. Want to go with me to the courthouse tomorrow?"

"Of course. I'll pick you up at eight. I don't have another hike scheduled until Friday. I'll call Mom tonight and pick her brain about this unknown great aunt of ours."

He nodded and shut the door, heading into his apartment building. A shiver went down my spine as the door closed behind him.

"Well, I hope it's safe. You didn't pick up anything, um, evil or anything about the book, right, Briar?"

I turned around to look at her, and she gave a kitty shrug before breaking eye contact and looking out the window.

"It felt neutral. I'm hungry. What's for dinner?"

"Oh, could we have some chicken?" Finn asked as she joined me in the front seat. "I love chicken."

"The human kind, not the slop in a can," Briar added, purring at the end.

"Noted. I'll swing by the grocery store and see what I can find."

A sense of surreal joy filled my heart as I left the parking lot and headed to the store. I had so many questions about Euphemia and this so-called magic, but I wasn't about to knock it. Not for one moment.

Chapter Six

By the time we made it back to the cabin, I was completely ravenous. I opened the back door, and Finn leapt out, racing around my legs, eyes full of joy. She did this every time we got back from a long car ride, but this was different. Now I could hear what she was saying.

"Free, free, free. I'm free to run. Hooray!"

Briar leapt down and stretched, arching her back and digging her claws into the gravel on my driveway.

"Ah, that feels good. That chicken smells delicious. When are we going to eat it?"

I grabbed the grocery bag from the back seat, the empty lunch bag I'd brought, and the carved wooden box.

"Soon. I just need to get everything in the house. Finn, did you want to go for a run?"

"Wheeeeeeeeeee!"

Her voice tapered off as she ran towards the back of the cabin. Briar fell in beside me as we walked up to the front door at a much more sedate pace. Finn tore around the side of the cabin, ears tucked back, her tail straight out behind her, and Briar chuckled.

"She needs a few more laps. Let's go in."

"Wheeeeeeee!!!!!"

The huge smile on my face stayed put as I unlocked the door and let Briar in. I'd always known there was nothing Finn loved more than running flat out, but now I could hear her joy and it made my day. My year, even. I put the grocery bag on the counter and the cat immediately jumped up, rooting through the plastic. I put the wooden box out of the way, where it wouldn't get any food on it.

"Hey, I'm coming. Give me a second to get a plate."

A scratching sound came from the door and I opened it, revealing Finn, sitting there with a big doggy grin. She bounced inside, tail wagging.

"That was amazing. Thank you."

"And thank you for not running off. I always worry about that."

She paused mid-step and turned towards me, brown eyes serious.

"Oh, Tessa. We would never leave you. Would we, Briar?"

"Nope. You're stuck with us. We picked you, you know. At the shelter. We saw you come in, and we just knew you were the one. Quite a few people wanted to adopt Finn, but they weren't interested in a cat. We knew the right person wouldn't mind us both."

My throat clogged with emotion as I walked back to the kitchen and stared at my cat. I reached out, stroking the soft fur on her back.

"Really? You picked me?"

"Chicken, Tessa. Priorities."

I grabbed the rotisserie chicken out of the bag and pulled off the lid. Finn's eyes got big as I began pulling the meat off the bone for both of them.

"What pulled the two of you together in the shelter? I remember the lady who worked there thought it was the strangest thing."

Finn and Briar shared a look, and the cat shook her head slightly.

"That's a story for another day. A day when we're all cuddled up, safe and warm. That is not a tale for a day when the sun is shining and we've been blessed with a rare gift."

I swallowed hard and nodded, going back to my task. Before long, their bowls were full, and I had enough chicken and fixings left to make up a nice little dinner for myself. Instead of taking my plate to the tiny, two-person table I usually sat at, I leaned against the counter and ate with them.

"This is so good," Finn said, in between bites. "Thank you, Tessa. You're the best."

Briar said nothing, but it was clear from the way she was scarfing up the chicken that she was enjoying her treat, too. I polished off my food in record time and piled the dishes into the sink. I glanced at the towel hanging down from the cabinet under the sink and shook my head.

"I still can't believe Paul's the one who ruined that towel. Well, at least I know. I'll have to make us a new one."

"Oh, maybe you could make me a new toy?" Finn asked, her tail brushing the floor as she wagged it back and forth. "I loved the one you made me before. I'm sorry I got a little carried away and shredded it."

She hung her head and her tail stopped moving. I stroked her head softly.

"Hey, it's okay. I love making stuff. I'll make you both something special. Now, you can pick your colors and patterns. We'll have fun with it."

That lifted her mood, and she was back to smiling, skipping a little as she headed for the couch.

"Come on, Briar. Let's see if that squirrel is in the yard. I know how much you like watching him."

My cat paused, one foot in the air, and looked at me. If I wasn't mistaken, she was a tad embarrassed by Finn's revelation. I chucked her under the chin and nodded towards the living room.

"Go ahead. I've got to do these dishes and then call my mom."

She leapt down from the counter and joined Finn in the living room, both staring out the big bay window into the woods beyond. Once I had the dishes done, I dried my hands and leaned against the counter. I didn't know what to expect from this call I was going to make, and my hands felt a little sweaty.

"This is crazy. I call my mom all the time. Just do it, Tessa."

I checked the time on the microwave. If I was going to call my folks, I'd need to do it soon. They were two hours ahead of our time and I knew they liked to go to bed early, preferring to be up with the sun, much like I did. I let out a breath and nodded, grabbing my phone.

My mom picked up on the second ring.

"Tessa! I didn't expect to hear from you today. How's everything back home?"

The familiar sound of her voice helped me relax a fraction, and I leaned against the counter.

"Good. How's everything in sunny Florida?"

"Rainy," my mom said, laughing. "But it's supposed to be a scorcher tomorrow. How's your brother?"

I glanced at the wooden box and jumped in with both feet.

"He's fine. We had an interesting day, actually."

"Really? What happened?"

I ran my finger over the carving of the cat and dog on the box and gathered my inner strength.

"Do you remember Euphemia Hawthorne?"

Silence filled the line and I could almost see my mom's face. She'd be blinking and running a hand through her shoulder length hair while she gathered her thoughts. Just like Paul did.

"Should I?"

"Well, considering she's our great aunt, probably. We each got a letter from a courier today and went to meet with her lawyer."

My mom bit back a sharp gasp and I heard her move the phone away, likely covering it with her palm. I still heard her call for my father, though.

"Timothy!"

"What?"

A smile quirked my lips at his cranky tone. He was probably watching the evening news, like he had my entire life. He loved to park himself in his favorite recliner, watch the news, and head to bed as soon as it was over. Any serious discussion had to wait until after the news finished, or preferably, for the next morning.

"This is important."

I heard the mechanism of his recliner and a groan. He joined my mother and I could hear them whispering in the background.

"You need to talk to her."

"What's all this about?"

"Just do it, Tim."

"Fine. Geez Louise, Denise, you don't have to shove the phone at me. Hi pumpkin, what's shaking? How's that brother of yours?"

"Good. We learned about our great aunt Euphemia today."

A clatter sounded on the other end of the call and I winced as I realized he'd dropped my mom's cellphone. A shriek in the background confirmed it.

"Tim! Oh, is the screen cracked?"

"It's fine. Hang on a second. Pumpkin, are you still there?"

"I'm here, dad. What's going on?"

"I'd almost forgotten about her. It's been, heck, probably forty years since I'd heard that name. How on earth did you, I mean..."

"She died, dad. She had a lawyer reach out to us. We visited him today. She left us a few things..."

"Tessa, I'm sorry she's dead, but there was always something different about her. Wrong. I can't believe she had someone contact you. She promised me. Whatever she gave you, I'd get rid of. I'm not kidding."

A chill slithered down my spine at his words. I didn't know what to say, and stood there for a moment, mouth open. Briar must have sensed something was wrong, and she trotted my way, tail held high. Finn followed and leaned against my leg, lending me support.

"She left a letter. She said that now that she was dead, she was no longer bound by that promise. She gave Paul an old book, and the deed to a property. We haven't gone to look at it yet."

"What did she leave you?"

I paused, hesitant. Typically, I could tell my father anything, but something made me hold my tongue.

"A carved wooden box. It's beautifully made."

He paused and cleared his throat.

"Well, that's alright, then. Look, I know I'm probably coming off harsh, but that side of the family was always a little strange. We thought it was just hippie nonsense, but Euphemia believed in it. I don't know what to tell your brother, but I'd probably sell whatever she left him and be done with it. Throw away that box, pumpkin. It's probably cursed. I don't want to talk about this again. She's been dead to me for decades and that's where she'll stay."

His tone left no room for argument and I heard my mom bite back a gasp.

"Well, she was odd. I never liked her. You didn't like her, either, Denise, so don't play innocent. You thought she was a witch."

"Give me that phone, Tim. There's no need to be rude. The poor woman is dead."

"Alright, fine. Goodnight, pumpkin. Take my advice, okay?"

My mom's voice came back on the line, but my mind was a million miles away from whatever she was saying. At least I had confirmation that Euphemia was probably magical, but I didn't know if it was a good thing. I shook my head and interrupted my mom.

"I know it's late there, Mom. I should let you go. I'll call next week, okay?"

"Okay, sweetheart. I'd listen to your father, though. He knows what he's talking about. I never liked that side of the family. They were just..."

"It's fine, mom. Goodnight."

I signed off the call and put my phone down next to the box. My fingers were drawn to it, despite what my father said. Briar put a soft paw on top of my hand and I met her eyes.

"It doesn't feel evil," she said, her voice gentle. "If that's what you're worried about. And the magic you carry in your blood isn't evil. We all make choices, every single day. For good and bad. I know you, Tessa. You'll make the right choices."

"Briar's right. You're the best human I've ever known. If there's anyone who would be safe to leave that kind of power to, it's you."

I didn't know what to say after that ringing endorsement. I could only hope that I'd live up to their faith in me.

"Well, so far, the only thing that seemed to happen is the ability to talk to you two, so I'm not too worried. And there's no way I'm giving that back. This is the best thing that's ever happened to me."

"That's more like it," Briar said, purring softly. "Now, let's go watch some television and cuddle on the couch. We always do that after dinner and it's good for digestion. Maybe we can call it an early night, too."

They ushered me into the space I called my living room, but in reality, it was just a few feet away from the kitchen. I took my usual spot on the couch as they arranged themselves around me. As always, Briar took the spot on my lap, and Finn laid next to me on the other couch cushion.

"Anything in particular you'd like to watch?" I asked as I flipped the remote in my hand.

"Hmmm. How about a game show? I always like that trivia one. It stretches the brain. I always try to see how many questions I can answer."

Finn huffed softly.

"Fine, but after that, I want to watch a baseball game. I love imagining I'm out there, fielding the ball."

Contentment stole through my veins as I relaxed back on the couch. My parents had to be wrong. My eyes grew heavy as Briar purred contentedly in my lap and Finn nestled close, her head a comforting weight on my feet. Nothing bad could come from a gift like this.

Chapter Seven

Stars glittered overhead, and the moon gleamed like a jewel set in a shadowy crown as I walked up a path I'd traveled many times. A breeze filtered through the trees, raising the hair on my arms. A sensation of being utterly lost swamped my senses. I hadn't felt this way in years. If ever. My feet slid on the trail, and my stomach lurched as I went down, landing hard.

A whimpering sound echoed through the darkness and it took me a second to realize I was the one making that sound. Footsteps sounded behind me and I struggled to get to my feet as fear spiked through my veins, its edges jagged and painful. A voice sounded behind me, dark and full of menace.

"I'm coming for you. You won't get away. You know the saying, you can run but you cannot hide? I'm sure you do, little one."

Little one? No one had called me that in years. Since I'd been a child. I wasn't the tallest person in my family. That honor went to Paul, who stood at a little over six feet. But I was five foot eight on a good day, and a little taller in my boots. Who was speaking? I'd never heard that voice in my life.

My feet kept moving, even though I wondered about the voice and wanted to stay, let them catch up to me and see who they were.

It was as if I wasn't in control of my body. I hurried up the trail, searching for somewhere, anywhere, I could hide.

"I'm coming. You won't get away."

Revulsion roiled through me as I slipped yet again, coming down hard on a knee and my hands. My palms stung, but my knee shrieked in agony, slowing me down. The footsteps got closer and my heart rate zoomed, blood pumping in my ears.

I had to get away. I didn't know who this person was, but it was obvious they meant me harm. Realization hit that I was alone. Truly alone. Finn and Briar were nowhere to be found. My chest hitched as I glanced behind me. There, about fifteen feet back, a man was steadily gaining on me, his features shrouded in the night shadows. He was tall, broad shouldered, and wore evil like a cloak. That whimpering noise ripped from my mouth as I began scrambling upward again, the gravel biting into the soles of my feet.

A laugh pealed behind me and my heart nearly stopped in dread as my feet refused to cooperate. To move faster. I'd hiked this trail at least once a month. I knew it like the back of my hand. But I'd never climbed it at night. Why was I here? Who was the man behind me?

"Almost there, little one. Just a little further."

I forced my legs to keep moving, even though my hair fell in my face, blinding me as the curls tangled in the sudden gust of wind. I brushed them aside and surged forward. I was going to make it. I was going to find a safe spot to hide, to get away from this madman. He would not catch me.

The stones underneath my feet rolled, dropping me again, my hands bruised and aching as they broke my fall. Powerlessness flooded my senses as I struggled to get to my feet, knee aching. A hand closed around my ankle with an iron grip and I shrieked as I felt myself yanked backwards, the man's smell overwhelming my senses.

"Tessa! Wake up! You're dreaming. Stop this!"

I bolted upright, heart pounding in my chest. A soft glow from the television cast enough light to let me see I'd fallen asleep on the couch. Finn was staring at me, her eyes wide in the dark, while Briar growled low in her chest, fur spiked in every direction. I took a ragged breath. And then another one.

"Was I screaming?" I asked, running my hands through my hair, catching a finger on the ponytail holder I'd left in. "Wow, that was a horrible nightmare."

I pulled the elastic out of my hair as a jolt of realization hit me. In the dream, I'd had curly hair. My hair was straight. It wouldn't hold a curl no matter how hard I tried. Why had my hair been curly in the dream? I shook off the thought as I realized both of my pets were staring at me.

"You've never made a sound like that before," Briar said, her voice pitched low. "We didn't know what to do. You wouldn't wake up."

"Are you... are you okay, Tessa?" Finn asked, shoving her cold nose underneath my hand. "You scared me."

"I'm so sorry, you two. I don't remember ever having a dream that bad in my life."

I pulled my knees up to my chest and rolled my neck, working out the kink I'd gained from falling asleep at a weird angle. My heart rate slowly returned to normal as I took in my surroundings. The night sky was still black, but a slight glow warmed the edges of the horizon to the east. The sun would be up in about an hour. I'd slept most of the night on the couch.

Briar set to work, putting her fur to rights, while Finn whined, the worried sound going straight to my heart. I ran my fingers through the fur behind her ears, finding that favorite spot of hers that always made her grin in delight.

"I'm okay, guys. I'm sorry I scared you. I'm going to make some coffee. There's no way I'm gonna be able to go back to bed after that."

I padded into the kitchen, followed by my two friends, and set to work making coffee. The familiar ritual soothed the last vestiges of fear from my mind and I felt almost normal as the coffee began dripping into the pot. Briar jumped on the counter and brushed my arm with her fur.

"Do you want to talk about it?"

I thought for a moment. So many things in the dream felt familiar. It felt so real somehow. So incredibly real. I turned over my hand, expecting to see it filled with abrasions and bits of gravel.

"It was so real," I said, breathing out as I lowered my unmarked palm. "I was on the Ridgeline Trail. You know the one, it's my most popular hike. I've got a group going there this weekend."

I trailed off, blinking. Had the dream been a warning? Was something bad going to happen on my hike? But no, the dream was set at night and I never led groups on that trail in the dark. It was simply too dangerous. I shook my head. They exchanged glances before Briar pinned me with a green-eyed glare.

"Go on."

I described the rest of the dream, rubbing my hands on my arms to get rid of the chill that seemed to permeate my very bones. I poured a cup of coffee and wrapped my fingers around the mug.

Briar was quiet while Finn shuffled her feet on the floor, her worried eyes never leaving mine. The silence hung heavily while I sipped my coffee.

"I think your gift is more than just talking to us," Briar said finally, before turning to nip at her flank.

"What do you mean?"

It took her a moment as she licked her fur back into place. I knew her well enough to know that you didn't rush Briar, but I tapped my fingers on my mug as I waited, impatient for her to speak again.

"I think you somehow got access to someone's memories as they were being killed. There were too many details for it to be random. Too many things that make little sense for it to fit something your subconscious would dream up. From him calling you little one, to the curly hair. No, I think you were dreaming about someone else."

I gripped the mug so hard I nearly broke it.

"That just can't be. Can it? What if I could have stopped it? Maybe it hasn't happened yet. Maybe I was given the dream to keep it from happening. I could call Jace..."

I trailed off as I grimaced. Jason Roberts was a local sheriff's deputy, and my ex-boyfriend. We'd dated in high school, and for a little while we were in college, but it hadn't ended well. I'd just dealt with him a few weeks ago during the hike where I'd met Eden and Hannah. Thanks to them, we'd solved the murder before he could, and I was certain he was still unhappy about that.

Finn wagged her tail, the movements uncertain.

"Or we could go look. I can help you look for a body. We already helped solve a murder. We can do it again!"

I narrowed my eyes as I looked between them, realization dawning.

"You two helped Eden and Hannah, didn't you? That's how they knew Darlene Prescott had been killed, isn't it?"

"Well, it mostly Briar," Finn said, her tail slowing. "I think they can only talk to cats. They didn't understand me."

"Razzy and Gus were very helpful, but yes, we played a role in bringing her killer to justice. I'd almost forgotten about that with the rush of discovering we could communicate with you now."

I wondered briefly just how little I knew about these two pets of mine. What else had they done when I couldn't understand them? As it was, it was clear they were extremely bright, which, of course, I'd always known, but their intelligence bordered on downright frightening.

"Do you know where you were in the dream when you went down on the trail? If something happened, we can start there and see if we can find anything."

I nodded and drained my mug, looking out the bay window that faced the forest. We just had another half hour and the sun would be up. I could run out to the trail and see if it had really just been a dream. If I hurried, I could even make it back to town in time to go with Paul to the courthouse. I had to know. I needed to see if it really had been just a dream.

"Let's do it. It's better than sitting here wondering about it. I'll take you outside, Finn, and then I'll get ready and we'll go. It's only about a half hour drive from here, and if we hustle, we can be at the midway point in another thirty."

Finn spun around in a circle, her feet moving so fast she was practically a black and white blur. Briar watched the dog's antics with a soft smile before nodding at me.

"Better bring some coffee for the road. I have a feeling you're gonna need the extra caffeine."

I rinsed my mug in the sink and grabbed a travel mug. She was right. Now that the terror had loosened its grip on my mind, I felt a little fuzzy around the edges. Coffee would certainly help that. Either I'd dreamt about an actual murder, or my mind was just working overtime and on the fritz, given what had happened yesterday. Maybe the lightning bug had fried my brain. I shelved that thought as I walked outside with Finn and waited for her to do her business.

Briar sat with me, her tail brushing my leg as she waved it back and forth. Finn was engaging in her morning zoomies.

"She's such a sweet soul, isn't she?"

"She is. Someday, I want to hear about how the two of you linked up in the shelter."

"You will. Someday. For today, bring your gun. I know you don't enjoy carrying it, but I don't want you, well, us, going in unprotected."

I nearly swallowed my tongue as I looked down at my cat. When I'd started my hiking business, I'd applied for and received a permit to carry concealed. Mountain lions and other predators were a reality on the trails, and while I'd never had to shoot one, and hoped I never did, being prepared was important. I nodded slowly, seeing her point.

"Okay. I'll put it in my pack."

She yowled, making me jump, and I watched as Finn skidded to a stop in the field nearby and came tearing back, her tail straight behind her as she raced in our direction.

"That's a handy trick. I wish I'd known you could do that back when I was training Finn to listen to my voice commands."

Her little black and white face was the picture of innocence.

"Oh yes. Training. As if we didn't already know what to do. Sometimes humans make me chuckle."

She entered the house as Finn skittered to a stop on the porch, sliding the last few feet. Her tongue lolled out of her mouth and she looked much more joyful.

"Better get a drink. I'll bring your portable water bowl, too. It's gonna be another hot one today."

I closed the screen door behind her and looked outside, unable to shake the feeling that I was about to discover something horrible out there on that trail. Something that would change our lives forever. I swallowed hard and turned. Whatever it was, I had to be ready.

Chapter Eight

By the time we reached the trailhead, the sun was fully up and it was shaping up to be a beautiful day. A light breeze snaked through my hair as I got out of the car and let Finn and Briar out. They stuck close, their eyes wide as they looked around. Ours was the only vehicle in the lot, but that didn't mean we were alone out here.

I knelt down and secured Finn's harness around her narrow shoulders. No matter how much I fed this dog, she remained whipcord lean. Her vet assured me she was perfectly healthy, and now that I could ask Finn myself, I'd make it a point to ensure she was never hungry. Briar's harness came next, a formality that I'm sure she put up with entirely to appease my overly protective nature.

"You can always ride in my pack if you get tired, Briar," I said, clipping on the thin lead to the buckle on her harness.

"Yeah, yeah. Finn will let me catch a ride if I need one. That's way more fun than being trapped on all sides by fabric."

I glanced down at Finn's harness, glad I'd gone with the one that had wide straps. I'd been accidentally clawed by Briar in the past, and couldn't imagine her sinking her claws through Finn's thin and wiry fur. At least with the harness, Briar would have something to grip to.

I shouldered my pack, all too aware of the extra weight from the gun stowed in the bottom and closed the back door of the Land Rover.

"Okay, guys. I've got water in case you're thirsty and some snacks, too. Let's go."

"Geez, it's not like it's our first hike," Briar grumbled as she walked ahead of me.

Finn grinned over her shoulder and glanced at me.

"It's her love language, Briar. You know that. She likes to fuss over us and make sure we're cared for. You just like complaining. I think that might be your love language."

I bit my lip to keep from laughing at the look on Briar's face. Let's just say Finn wasn't wrong. Briar was a tad on the particular side. It was one of the many things I appreciated and loved about her. Finn was the easy one. Briar was the one who taught me patience, and just how deeply a cat can love if you give them a chance.

The lightness I was feeling inside faded as we headed up the trail, so similar to what I'd seen in my dream. Now, at least, I could see the rocks on the trail that threatened to turn an ankle. I checked the tree line, unable to shake the feeling that something was wrong.

"I sense a few people have been on this trail recently," Briar said, lashing her tail from side to side. "Probably in the past few hours."

"You can do that?" I asked, mouth open. "Do you have like a magical ability or something?"

Briar gave me a kitty eye roll.

"I can smell them, Tessa. You may not realize, but cats have a sense of smell that is just as powerful as a bloodhound. We can scent and track just like a dog can. Maybe even better."

Finn huffed from her spot a few feet ahead, but said nothing. Briar frowned, her little forehead wrinkling.

"Well, let's just say we're about equals in the smell department. Finn, what are you picking up?"

"A rabbit went through here a few minutes ago. He smells juicy. And fast."

Briar shot me a look and shook her head.

"Dogs. Any humans, Finn?"

"Oh, yes. A couple. The scents are hard to read, though. The dew has already evaporated, taking a lot of the smells with it."

My shoulders tightened as we rounded the corner on the trail and entered a familiar stretch.

"This is where my dream started. I felt lost. But I shouldn't have felt that way. I've lost count of the times I've been on this trail. It's one of my favorites."

My pets said nothing, but they both bent their heads, sniffing the trail intently. Finn raised her head and looked at me.

"I don't scent you at all. I know it's not possible, but I still wanted to check."

"It might be possible," Briar said, waving her tail. "She might have astral traveled here in her dream. That could be why it felt so real."

"But I don't think you'd leave your scent behind if you did that. Whatever it is. She wasn't here. That's all I meant. Physically, anyway."

My mind spun as I looked between them. Astral travel? How much did Briar know? She was turning out to be quite the source of information about magic. Why did she know so much? My thoughts were interrupted as a familiar pile of rocks came into view. I took a shuddering breath.

"Okay, this is where I heard his voice for the first time."

We were standing in full sun, but I felt cold to the bone as I looked behind me, half expecting to see the hulking form of the man in my dream standing there. Luckily, the trail was empty.

I spun back around and kept walking, taking my time as I looked at the stones on the trail, trying to remember if I'd seen any in my dream. About a hundred yards in the distance was the spot I'd fallen for the second time in my dream, scraping my hands. And just beyond that was the part where I'd fallen for the last time, when I felt his hand on my ankle. I glanced down at my foot, covered by a hiking boot, and realized that in my dream, I'd been barefoot. Weird.

Finn whined, her nose held high as she scented the air.

"What is it?"

"Over there. I smell something... well, there's no delicate way to put it. I smell something terrible."

Briar's fur fluffed as Finn's hackles raised, giving her a mohawk down her spine. She growled low in her chest as she dropped her head and moved forward. I followed, legs numb, as she led me into the trees that bordered the trail.

She halted and turned her sorrowful eyes towards me.

"She's right there. You were right, Tessa. Your dream was right."

My brain went fuzzy as I stared at the sole of a foot underneath a bush. A bare foot. I didn't need to look closer to know that it belonged to a woman. I didn't need to see that she had curly hair. My dream had a been a vision, and I'd experienced this poor woman's death.

My hand was surprisingly steady as I pulled my phone out of my side pocket and checked for service. I had two bars. Just enough to place a call. I dialed 9-1-1 and waited. A woman's voice came on the line and words spilled out of my mouth almost faster than I could think of them.

"Hello? I'm on the Ridgeline Trail about halfway up and I just found a body in the woods. She isn't moving."

"Alright, sweetie. I've got your location. Please describe what happened."

The no-nonsense tone of the woman on the other end of the call settled my nerves. I rattled off a heavily redacted version of the events, leaving out, of course, my wild dream.

"Have you checked to see if she's injured?"

I didn't want to touch this poor woman, but what if the dispatcher was right? What if she wasn't dead? I gathered my strength and looked at Finn. She shook her head slightly. But I needed to see for myself.

"One second. I'm touching her foot."

The coldness of the woman's skin is a sensation I'll never forget.

I pulled my hand away as though it was burned. Tears slid down my cheeks.

"She's dead. I touched the bottom of her foot. I didn't want to disturb the body too much."

"All right, miss, we've got a unit on their way to your location now. I'm going to need you to stay put. What's your name, honey?"

"Tessa Windsor. What's yours?"

"Tina. The deputy will arrive at the trailhead in about five minutes. Can you describe the condition of the body?"

I swallowed hard and nodded, even though Tina couldn't see me.

"I can't see much of her. Just a foot. The rest of her is covered in brush. I'm hiking with my dog and she's the one who led me over this way. You can't see anything from the trail."

"Okay. Are you from Collinsville?"

"Born and raised. How about you?"

If she thought it was odd that I was asking her personal questions, she didn't mention it. I just needed to get my mind off the dead body at my feet. I stepped a few feet away, out of the shade of the trees, and felt the sun warm my skin. Finn trotted after me, her tail hanging low, while Briar sniffed around the scene, placing each paw deliberately so she wouldn't disturb anything.

"I'm from South Dakota. I moved here a few years ago. What kind of dog do you have?"

"She's a border collie. I've got my cat along too. She likes to hike with us."

"Well, isn't that cute? I've got a little chihuahua I bring to work with me. She's at my feet right now."

I realized Tina was a pro. She was distracting me from the horror of my discovery and keeping my mind going.

"What's her name?"

"Baby. She's about two pounds, soaking wet. I used to run a dog rescue in the small town where I'm from. We had a few border collies we placed. Is yours a tornado of activity?"

"Sometimes. She's very well behaved, though. She comes with

me on all of my hikes. Briar, the cat, does too. They're quite the team."

I heard someone coming up the trail and moved closer to it, shading my eyes from the sun as I tried to make out who it was. I couldn't help but frown when I recognized the blocky frame of the man approaching. I hadn't been lucky enough to get a different deputy.

"Jace is here, Tina. Thanks for talking with me."

"Okay, honey. You stay safe out there."

I slid the phone in my pocket and crossed my arms over my chest as Jace Roberts approached, slightly out of breath, and red faced. His eyes were anything but friendly as they met mine. He wiped the sheen of sweat off his brow and nodded.

"Tessa."

"Jace."

It was a repeat of how we'd talked a few weeks ago when he'd responded to our call for help with Darlene Prescott.

"So, I…"

"What's going on?"

We spoke over each other and I flushed from the sheer awkwardness of the moment. Why did Jace have to be a deputy? And why did I continually have to keep running into him? He frowned and held up a hand.

"What happened?"

I took a steadying breath and pointed off the trail.

"I was hiking and Finn scented something. I followed her over there and discovered the body of a woman. You'll be able to see her foot when you approach. The rest of her is covered."

He pushed back his cowboy hat and gave me a long look.

"What are you doing up here?"

"Hiking."

"Alone? Where's your group?"

"It's just me today. I have a hike scheduled tomorrow."

He snorted and scratched the side of his nose.

"You hike on your off time? You're a glutton for punishment, aren't you?"

Memories of our disastrous relationship filtered through my mind and I bit my tongue to keep from saying something nasty. The problem was, he wasn't wrong.

"I like to stay active."

He shifted the duty belt under his belly and flushed a darker red before turning and heading towards the trees. Finn moved to follow, but I gently pulled on her lead.

"Not now. We'll only go over there if he wants us to."

Finn nodded, her tail gently wagging, while Briar sat near my feet. She muttered just loud enough that I could hear her over the wind filtering through the pines.

"What on earth did you ever see in that guy?"

"Don't start," I hissed, not needing a reminder of the gripping insecurity of my high school years.

Jace knelt by the body and moved the brush aside. I didn't want to look, but some part of me had to know. I walked a few steps and stood on my toes to get a better line of sight. I spotted a hank of long, red, curly hair and my stomach clenched. It was just like the hair I'd seen in the dream. I stepped back, stunned.

"Call Paul," Briar said, her tail brushing my calf. "He should be here."

I nodded and fished my phone back out, tapping on Paul's contact name. He answered on the first ring.

"Morning, Tess. You on your way over?"

"Oh gosh, that's right. The courthouse. Actually, no, Paul. I'm on the Ridgeline Trail. Can you get over here? I found a body. Jace is already here."

Paul let out a very colorful string of swear words, but I could hear him moving in the background and the tinkle of the keys he grabbed. A loud sneeze followed.

"On my way. How far up are you?"

"About a mile or so."

"I'll be there."

He ended the call, and I stowed my phone as Jace looked at me, eyes narrowed. He motioned for me to walk in his direction.

"Yes?"

"Who were you calling?"

"Paul. Why?"

"Just what we need. The press. It couldn't wait?"

"He's coming as my brother, not as the editor of the paper, Jace. Geez."

He had the good grace to look away, but I knew the moment wouldn't last. We seemed to exist solely to irritate one another. He pointed down at the body and looked at Finn.

"Pretty impressive that she caught the scent. This woman hasn't been dead for long. You're certain that's what happened?"

I nodded and wrapped Finn's leash around my hand.

"Yeah. She woofed and headed over here. She's well trained, so I knew it had to be important. She doesn't leave the trail on a whim."

He nodded and took off his hat, striking it against his beefy thigh.

"Well, she didn't die of natural causes. This woman was strangled. Did you see anyone around on the trail when you were coming up?"

I shook my head as a chill went down my spine. I hadn't even thought of that. What if my dream had been in real time? Good lord, we might have stumbled across the killer on our mad rush up here.

"No. No one was around."

"Alright. Well, I need to get the crime scene techs out here. Head on back to the trailhead and wait around for a bit, would you? I might have some more questions."

Dismissed, I nodded again and backed away, grateful to be away from the body and back in the sunlight. Finn slowed and Briar leapt on her back, steadying herself by sinking her claws into the canvas harness. We headed back to the trailhead, lost in our thoughts. My dream had been way more than just a dream, but I didn't know what to do with the information. We'd helped find the woman's body, but how were we going to find her killer? I walked faster, trying to outrun my swirling thoughts.

Chapter Nine

I propped open the back door of the Land Rover and leaned against the bumper while waiting for Paul. We'd made it back to the trailhead in record time, but it was clear both Finn and Briar were tired. I was, too, and put it down to lack of sleep and an incredibly stressful morning. I still couldn't believe we'd found a body.

Finn lounged on her padded mat in the back of the Rover while Briar perched on the headrests of the seat behind her. Finn's ears swiveled, and she stopped panting, her eyes keen as she looked beyond me, to the east of the trailhead.

"What?"

"Shhh. She's listening," Briar said.

I bit back a retort and followed Finn's sightline until I saw someone threading their way through the woods. They were too far away to see clearly, but the person was tall, most likely male, and carrying a brightly patterned backpack. I squinted, hoping to spot the man's face, but couldn't. He kept going, past the trailhead, towards the road beyond.

"Well, that was weird, right?" Briar asked once the man was gone.

"You don't think it was the killer, do you?" Finn asked, her voice breathless. "Should we track him? We know what direction he was going. We could catch up to him."

Her paws twitched, and I laid my hand on her head.

"No. I don't think that's a good idea. It might be just someone backpacking their way through. And if it is the killer, I don't think the three of us want to tangle with him. I never saw his face in my dream, but I'll never forget the way he smelled. It was terrible."

"That's new," Briar said, perking up, her ears swiveling my way. "What do you mean?"

"It just came back to me," I said, staring down at my boots while feelings swamped me. "In the dream, when he grabbed my, well, the woman's ankle, I caught his smell. It was like BO and something else. Something musty."

"So, we're looking for a murderous hippie who doesn't like to bathe. Was it patchouli that you smelled?"

A small smile curled the edges of my lips as I shook my head.

"No. Not patchouli. I don't know how to describe it, but if I ever smelled it again, I'd know who it was in a heartbeat. No, I'll tell Jace we spotted him, but we're not going after that person on our own. Besides, they're probably a through-hiker. We get a lot of those in this area."

Finn let out a sharp bark and then shot me an embarrassed look.

"Sorry, but Paul just pulled in. That bark slipped out."

I ruffled her fur and grinned at her.

"You never need to apologize to me, sweetheart," I said, as I waved at Paul.

He whipped his old Nissan pickup into the space next to mine and was outside of the rig almost before the engine shut off. He looked at Jace's pickup and back towards me.

"Why are you standing out here alone? Where the heck is Jace? If there's a murderer around, you could have been targeted next!"

I put a hand on his arm, interrupting his rant.

"Paul, I'm okay. I'm not alone. I've got these two with me. And I'm armed. I'm not taking any chances."

He let out a breath and ran a hand through his tousled hair. It was standing on end in places, and I was certain he'd been tearing at it during the drive over here.

"Tell me what happened. From the beginning. Why are you even out here this morning? This isn't your usual routine. What's going on, Tess? I'm going crazy over here."

I glanced up the trail to make sure Jace wasn't heading our way.

"Okay, I need you to stay calm. Last night, well, early this morning, I guess, I had a dream. I guess it wasn't a dream, though. It must have been a vision or something similar. It's hard to describe…"

"Try. What do you mean, a vision?"

"I dreamt I was here on this trail, in the dark. I was barefoot, and a man was chasing me. He grabbed me and that's when I screamed and woke these guys up, and then they woke me up. It felt so real, Paul. So, I knew I had to come out here. The person in the dream wasn't me, but it felt like it was. It was the most surreal thing. Anyway, I came out here to see if it was true. Right in the spot where I fell in the dream is where we discovered the body. Jace said she hasn't been dead for very long. I could've stopped it, Paul. What if I'd come sooner? Right when I had the dream? Is it my fault she's dead?"

Finn let out a low howl and crowded close, pushing her nose under my armpit, while Briar lashed her tail. Paul's face had gone nearly white underneath his tan.

"Tessa… I…"

"There's nothing you could've done," Briar said, her tone serious as she stared at me. "I don't think that's why you received that vision. I think you had it because we need to catch the man. Stop him from killing again. But what happened was already in motion. If it hadn't been for you discovering her so quickly, the evidence would've disappeared. If we can trust Jace to collect it all. I still want to go up there once the body is gone."

Paul looked between us, but it was too much for me to translate all at once. Instead, I nodded as Briar's words sunk in.

"You're right, Briar. Sorry, it just all hit me at once. Paul. she thinks I saw what happened for a reason. I think she might be right. Oh, here are the crime scene techs. And the wagon."

A white van cruised in behind the squad car and I swallowed hard. They'd be collecting the woman's body and taking it back to town. Did she have ID on her? Would Jace be able to find her identity? What about her family? So many questions swirled in my head it nearly made me dizzy.

Paul watched them and waved at a tech as the group walked by.

"That's Simon. He's a good dude. Don't tell anyone, but he feeds me tips when the sheriff's office is being closemouthed. Jace is still up there?"

"Yep. He asked me to stay in case he has other questions. I'm sorry, this is keeping you from going to the courthouse. I might be here for hours, Paul. You can go back to town. I shouldn't have had you come all the way out here."

He held up a finger and scowled.

"One, you're my sister. I will always come running when you need something. Two, this is the twenty-first century. I've already sent a scanned copy of the deed over to the courthouse. They're searching the records and they'll get back to me with an address as soon as they have it. Geraldine already told me I might need to hire a locksmith if the place has been vacant for a while. There might not be any keys and the only owner on record was Euphemia."

I processed that information as the coroner's team took a gurney out of the back of the van. A black bag was tucked under one strap and my heart hurt as I watched them lift it over the curb and head up the trail. I didn't know why that woman was on the trail at night, but I'm certain she didn't know she'd be leaving it like this. I looked back at Paul and tried to smile, going back to what he'd said.

"That's great, Paul. I hope it's a good house. How nice would it be to get out of that apartment and spread out a little?"

"You know I need little space. The apartment is just fine. Besides, it might be a dump that needs to be condemned. Let's not get too excited."

"Or," I said, holding up a hand. "It might be a cool house with room for the library you've always wanted."

Paul's eyes lit and I could see the wheels as they turned. There was one sure-fired way to get my brother thinking. Mentioning libraries, books, or any combination thereof. That and anything to do with the newspaper business. Speaking of which...

"Are you going to write up a story about this?"

Paul chewed on his lip before nodding.

"Of course. I have to. I'll wait with you until Jace gets back. We'll need to keep her name out of it until her relatives are notified, if she has any. Do you think she was... I mean, did you recognize her?"

I shook my head as Paul twisted himself in knots, trying to ask the right question.

"No. I didn't recognize her. I saw little of her face, but I'd know that hair anywhere. Bright red and super curly. She'd stand out. I can easily say I've never seen her before."

He relaxed a fraction and breathed out a sigh.

"We'll just have to wait. Run me through that dream again. I want every detail."

Briar shifted on her perch as I propped my hip on the bumper and told my brother everything I remembered. Typically, with dreams, the longer I went from waking to talking about it, the more it faded. Not this dream, though. Everything remained crystal clear, as though it had been etched in my mind.

Paul noted a few things on his phone while I spoke. His face pulled into a frown. He glanced up at me, brown eyes full of worry.

"Why didn't you call me when you woke up? I would've come with you. I know I tease you a lot, Tess, but the thought of you heading out here, with just your cat and dog for protection..."

"Hey," Briar said, narrowing her eyes. "I'll have you know the two of us are elite level bodyguards."

"We'd let nothing happen to Tessa," Finn breathed, her eyes trained on Paul's face. "She's our everything."

"They're amazing," I said, past the lump in my throat at their words. "And I brought my gun. I didn't want to wake you, Paul. You've had precious little sleep lately, anyway. Let's not fight about it. Instead, we can fight over what Dad said last night."

Paul raised an eyebrow, and I nodded, folding my arms across my chest.

"You asked them about Euphemia?"

"I did. He knew exactly who she was, and apparently, there was no love lost there. Even Mom knew her. I guess they wrote her off as a crazy hippie witch and never got to know her. That's the vibe I got. Dad told me to throw away the box. I didn't tell them about the pet thing. I mentioned the book and the deed, though. I hope that was okay."

He shrugged and ran his hand through his hair again.

"It's fine. I have no plans to destroy the book. Unless I rip it trying to get the darn thing to open. It's the strangest thing. I tried using gentle steam last night, but it won't budge."

I glanced at my pets before looking at him.

"Maybe it's magic. Like the bug. It might not open until the timing is right. Or maybe there's something in the house that will unlock it."

Paul's eyes gleamed, but they dimmed quickly as he looked back towards the trail. His shoulders stiffened, and I didn't need to turn to know that Jace Roberts was headed our way. Paul never liked Jace, and once we'd broken up, he'd really disliked him.

I straightened up and put a steadying hand on Finn's head. She nuzzled close as Briar glared at the deputy.

"You wanna run your story by me again, Tess? I'm still having a hard time understanding why you were up here this morning."

Paul muttered something under his breath and Briar's whiskers twitched. Her keen ears must have picked it up. I wrestled my temper into submission and calmly explained why I'd come, sticking to the same story I'd told earlier.

He looked at Paul once I was finished and frowned.

"Lemme guess. You're gonna put this in the paper and scare the living daylights out of everyone, aren't you?"

"I think you mispronounced letting the public know about an actual threat to their safety, Jace. Of course I'm going to report on it. Do you have an identity yet?"

"No. She had nothing on her. No purse, no wallet. And if I did,

I wouldn't tell you anyway, Windsor. That's all for now, Tessa. I'll be in touch if I have more questions."

"But what about her..." I said, ignoring Paul's hand on my elbow. "What about her family? The people missing her?"

"We'll do our best to figure out who she is. If she's some transient, we may never know. As of right now, she's a Jane Doe, and that's all I can say. We'll run her prints, dental records, and DNA, but it might take a while to figure out her identity. You two can get out of here. They'll be bringing the body down shortly."

Part of me wanted to stay, to honor the woman who'd somehow been linked to me in her last moments. She'd lost her life on this trail, and I would not let it go. Not this easily.

Briar whispered so softly, I almost missed it.

"The guy in the woods."

"Oh! Jace. While I was waiting for Paul, I saw someone in the woods. They were right over there. It looked like a man, and he had a brightly colored pack. A Navajo pattern in blues and greens. He didn't stop, but I thought it was odd."

Jace rolled his eyes and turned away.

"Probably just a hiker. You two can go now."

I ground my teeth together while Paul glared at Jace. He glanced back towards me and raised his phone.

"I'll text you an address. We can meet there. I just got what we were waiting for."

Jace perked up. His eyes narrowed as he looked at us, but I closed up the back of the Rover and brushed past him while Paul went for his pickup. He would not get another word out of me. Not unless it would help the poor woman who'd been killed. Until then, we had a house to look at and plenty of things that needed to be figured out.

Chapter Ten

Paul's text came in before we'd left the trailhead, and I plugged the address into the GPS, just to be on the safe side. Finn grinned at me from the front seat, and I could just feel Briar staring at me from her spot on the backseat. I turned, narrowing my eyes as I backed out of my spot.

"What?"

"Have you ever wondered why you have such a great sense of direction on hikes, but once you're behind the wheel, it all flies out the window?"

I turned out of the parking lot, right on Paul's tail, and frowned.

"Hardee har har. I know I'm hopeless with driving places. I've always been that way."

"No, she's right," Finn said before putting her nose next to the vent in front of her and inhaling the cold air from the AC. "It's a little odd."

My feelings smarted a little as I tried to focus on the road. Paul had always made fun of me for my ability to get lost driving. And now my two best friends were joining in.

"Hey, you guys don't need to rub it in."

I felt the brush of Briar's soft paw on my arm, but refused to look back to meet her eyes as we headed down the highway.

"We're not being mean. I have a point."

"You usually do," I said, my mouth curling into a half smile. "What is it?"

"Remember when I said you had the capability for magic, but no spark? I think it has something to do with it."

Finn cocked her head to the side and looked at Briar.

"You know what? That makes sense. I never thought of that before. Great job, Briar. You're a genius."

I didn't need to look in the rearview mirror to confirm that Briar was preening under Finn's praise, but I did anyway. I have to admit, I wanted to see where she was going with this.

"Okay, and?"

"I'm getting to the point. Don't rush me. There's an art to telling a story, you know."

I bit my lip and tightened my grip on the wheel. I'd only been able to talk to my pets for a day, and already they were turning out to be characters. I should've known. I mean, they've always been hams. But hearing it somehow made it that much more real.

"Sorry. Go ahead."

"Well, as I was saying, despite your constant interruptions, you have the capability of magic. Likely, it was passed down by your aunt. Or maybe even on your mom's side. Do you have any witches on that side, do you think? Anyone with the sight, as you humans call it?"

I chewed on my lip and thought, but nothing came to mind. I shrugged and glanced in the rearview mirror.

"Not that I know of. Why?"

Briar heaved a sigh and Finn let out a huffing noise that sounded remarkably like a laugh.

"Get to the point, Briar. We're almost there."

"Fine. Your inability to navigate stems from the fact that you've broken your connection with the earth. When your feet are on the ground, the energy can flow through you. When you break that connection, you get lost. There."

I blinked a few times, and turned onto a side street, speeding up a little so I didn't lose Paul.

"Huh. That... Actually, that makes sense."

"Told you so."

I shook my head, glancing over at Finn.

"She enjoys saying that, doesn't she?"

"If you only knew."

I couldn't wait to learn more about these two. That they'd shared such rich communication between them, all the while I'd been oblivious, amazed me. I'd always known they were close, but now, hearing it directly from them, made it so much more real. My heart warmed as Paul pulled to a stop in a tree lined neighborhood. The only spot left behind him would've required me to parallel park, and let's just say the only thing worse than my navigation skills on wheels is the ability to park in small spaces. I steered the Land Rover a little further on and found a shady spot underneath a massive oak tree that towered over the street.

"All right guys. I'm guessing you want to go with?"

"Uh, yeah. Of course we do," Briar said, climbing into the front seat to wedge herself next to Finn. "You need us. What if there are magical traps? You might not sense them."

I frowned as I looked at them.

"Magic traps? And you can sense them?"

They glanced at each other, and Finn let out a low whine. Briar gave a kitty shrug and licked at her flank.

"Should be able to."

Her voice was muffled by the fur in her mouth and I got the feeling she wasn't terribly confident, but Paul was already standing at the door, waiting impatiently, so I let it slide.

"Okay, guys. You know the rules. When we're in town, you've got to be on your leashes."

Briar grumbled, but Finn let out a yip of pure joy as I fastened her lead onto her harness. Briar tilted her head so I could reach for her harness.

"This is entirely unnecessary. We won't run away."

"I know. But it's safer. And I don't want to pay a fine if we get got. Do you know how expensive that is?"

"No. We have little cares about humans and their rapaciousness."

I rolled my eyes as I clicked the lead onto her collar and opened the door. Paul was staring across the street as I got out, my tiny menagerie in tow.

"Which one is it?"

Paul pointed to a low-slung white house to our left, and I gasped, loudly. Finn looked around, her eyes instantly alert.

"What? What is it?"

"It's beautiful! I thought... Well, I thought it was going to be a run down Victorian house or something. I didn't expect... this."

"Neither did I," Paul said as we crossed the street and headed towards the house. "It's... amazing."

"It's beyond that. Way beyond."

This house, nestled in the older part of Collinsville, looked like it belonged somewhere in Santa Fe, New Mexico. Almost every surface was curved, and the entryway featured a curved glass block wall that sparkled in the sun. I walked towards it, leading Finn and Briar, almost as if I was in a dream.

The doors and window trim were painted black, but everything else was white or glass. My mouth hung open as I stopped at the front door and I turned to look at Paul.

"If you don't want this house, you're insane, and I'll gladly take it off your hands. Look at this place!"

My brother grinned, his eyes alight with surprise as he stood, hands on hips, looking around the property.

"Nah. You'd go crazy in a week. You love not having any close neighbors and having access to the wilderness right outside your door."

He was right, but I wasn't about to admit that point. I had serious house envy. My cabin was home, and I adored it, but this house? It was on a whole other level. Even the overgrown yard couldn't take away from its splendor. Paul wandered towards the front, where a large bay window looked out over the street.

I followed, kicking through the tall grass. I turned and scooped up Briar as Finn plunged ahead.

"I can do it," Briar said, twisting in my arms.

"I know you can. But I also know how much you love picking grass seeds out of your fur, and after a short walk through this, it would take you hours."

"Oh. Good point. Proceed."

I smothered a smile and joined Paul at the window, shifting Briar in my arms so I could peer inside. Paul glanced at me, more giddy than I'd ever seen him.

"Look at that furniture! It's pristine! Oh my gosh, it's like walking into an antique store and discovering the mother lode of mid-century modern furniture. I wish we'd known Euphemia. She had impeccable taste."

A touch of sorrow dampened my joy as I looked around at what we could see of the interior. Had Euphemia been lonely? She had to be. We were her only family, and Paul and I hadn't even known she existed.

"We can't get inside?"

"Geraldine at the county office said there was no lawyer on record, so they don't know who would have the keys. Everything is legit, though. I guess her will was on file with the county and everything looks good. It's going to take a couple of days to get everything sorted out, but I've got the all clear to call a locksmith."

I shook his arm and stared at him.

"So? Call one! Oh my gosh, I can't wait to see what's inside. This place is a gem. I don't think I ever noticed this house, and we grew up in this town."

"I already did, silly. I called one on my way over. He's supposed to meet me here in a couple of hours. I can't say I ever saw this place, either. How does everything look so nice? Euphemia had to be getting up there. The yard hasn't been mowed in weeks. I wonder if she did it herself or hired someone."

Briar squiggled in my arms and leaned closer to the window, sniffing, while Finn stared at her, brown eyes wide.

"Anything?" Finn asked, her ears held at half mast.

"I smell something," Briar said. "There's a hum of magic here. It smells like Paul and Tessa, though. Interesting."

I blinked and looked at the cat in my arms.

"What? How is that possible?"

"I think she keyed the magic protecting this house to her bloodline. You'll be able to enter, but no one else will. I wonder if the spell will fail once the door is open? Typically, magic can't sustain once the wielder dies."

I shot a glance at my brother, who was staring at me, and held up a finger.

"How do you know so much about magic, Briar? I mean, it just seems a little odd that you're this little fount of magical knowledge. Right when we need one."

She gave her typical kitty shrug and looked away.

"Funny how things work out, isn't it?"

I waited for her to elaborate, but she didn't. I shrugged and turned to Paul.

"Let's see if we can see inside any of the other rooms! I hope the neighbors don't think we're going to rob the place."

"Yeah, not the best way to meet your new neighbors," he said, looking around the houses.

"So you're gonna take it, right? You won't sell it?"

He grinned, and the years almost seemed to fall away from his face as he nodded.

"You bet I'm keeping it. If I ever wanted to design a house, it would look just like this one. It's like it was made for me."

He rounded the corner and Finn followed, dragging me forward. I took one last look at the front of the house and wondered if it had. Maybe Euphemia had known what each of us would like. My throat clogged with emotion as I caught up to my brother. The windows were too tall for me to see in, but he was craning his head up to peek inside. I leaned against the wall and waited, my thoughts drifting from our great aunt to the woman I'd found on the trail. If Paul's gift was made for him, what about mine?

"What are we going to do about the murder, Paul? I feel like I had that vision for a reason. Unless I'm going to suddenly get psychic flashes when someone is killed around here. My gosh, that would be awful. You don't think that's going to happen, do you?"

Briar shifted in my arms, pinning me with her green eyes.

"Everything happens for a reason. We just don't know what that reason is yet. Whatever happens, we're here for you, Tessa."

I stroked her soft fur and rested my chin on her fuzzy head while Paul gave me a serious look. Finn sat, resting one of her feet on my boot, like she always did, and a part of me eased at the familiar gesture. I gave him an awkward shrug.

"Sorry. I'm not trying to harsh your buzz about the house. We can talk about it later. I was just thinking about gifts and what mine might mean."

Paul patted my arm.

"It's fine, Tessa. The house is still going to be here. I can't see that much anyway, so I need to practice patience. Let's go sit on the front steps and brainstorm."

I nodded and led Finn back to the front of the house. Even though I'd never been to this place, somehow it felt like home as I sank down next to my brother on the concrete steps. I let Briar down, and she stretched out next to me, setting her fur back to rights, while Finn looked around the neighborhood, leaning against my knees.

"So, we need to figure out her identity. She might be a local, or she might have been visiting. Collinsville isn't that big, but it's big enough that it won't be easy."

"She had very distinctive hair. So red and curly. People would remember someone like her. I didn't..." I trailed off and swallowed hard. "I didn't see her face. I couldn't look, Paul. But that hair. Someone would know her by her hair."

He nodded and traced a pattern on the concrete between us.

"So, we need to ask around. Meggie knows most of the people in town. She could help."

I smiled at the mention of my best friend, well, my best human friend, and glanced at my watch. Meggie was probably getting ready for the lunch rush. If I wanted to talk to her, now was the best time. Paul must have followed my thoughts.

He elbowed me in the side and nodded towards my Land Rover.

"Go ahead. I'm gonna snoop around here while I wait for the locksmith. I can't wait to get inside and see what's in there."

"Be careful," I said as I stood, brushing off the back of my pants. "These guys were worried about magic traps."

Paul paled as he looked at Finn and Briar. My cat stretched, scraping her claws on the concrete.

"I think he'll be fine. It's familial magic. It will recognize him. I wouldn't go poking into deep dark corners when he's alone, though. Just in case."

Well, that was heartening. Sort of. I translated for my brother and he raised an eyebrow in a silent question.

"Yeah, I don't know how she knows so much, but hey, it's a good thing, right? Want me to say anything to Meggie for you?"

He shook his head and leaned back, stretching out his legs.

"Just hi is fine. Maybe you can bring me back some lunch. I could go for one of Meggie's green chile burgers."

If he'd realize how much Meggie loved him, and how perfect they were for each other, he could have that burger every day for free. But I bit my tongue and smiled. Now wasn't the time to continue my long campaign to bring the two of them together.

"Sounds good. See you soon."

We headed back to the Land Rover, Briar insisting that she could walk on her four legs just fine and didn't need to be carried. Finn huffed a sigh before leaping into her usual spot. Her eyes were bright as I started up the car. Paul wasn't the only one who loved Meggie's food. She always spoiled my pets whenever I brought them by and they knew very well some wonderful treats were in store.

Chapter Eleven

I parked behind the Robin's Roost and breathed a sigh of relief that the back patio was free of people. The clock on the dash said it was eleven, and Meggie didn't open until noon, but sometimes, people liked to show up early and snag a coveted patio table.

"Alright, guys. Let's go see what Meggie's up to."

Finn was out of the car as soon as I moved out of my seat and Briar was right behind her, the lead still attached to her collar. She gave me an impatient look as I grabbed my bag.

"Come on!"

"Coming. Coming. Hey, if I don't grab my wallet, no treats for us, so be patient, Briar."

She gave me a sassy paw flick and headed for the patio as I shut the Land Rover's door. The patio was in the perfect spot to catch the afternoon sun. The umbrellas were already up, to deflect the worst of the sun on a hot day, and the colorfully painted furniture looked inviting as we passed by, Finn's nails clicking on the wooden patio.

I stuck my head in the open back door of the restaurant and hollered for my friend.

"Meggie! You around?"

"Back here!" came the answering shout. "Hiya, Tess. I wasn't expecting you today. One second."

I couldn't let Finn and Briar follow me back into the kitchen, so I waited at the door until my friend appeared. Her black, curly hair was gathered up in a high ponytail and she looked as gorgeous as ever. Just seeing her made me feel better, and emotion I hadn't realized I was stifling threatened to expel itself all over everything. I clamped my lips shut, trying my best not to burst into tears.

Meggie looked at me closely, grabbed an arm, and steered all of us towards the closest table. I plopped down onto a cushioned seat as tears streamed down my face. Finn leaned close, whining softly as Briar hopped into the chair next to me, her little face full of concern.

"Tessa, what's wrong? What happened? I've never seen you like this. Oh gosh, did something happen to Paul?"

Her red cheeks went white as she reached for my hand. I shook my head and tried on a smile that felt very shaky.

"He's fine. It's just... Wow, I don't even know where to start."

"Sit right there," she said, putting a hand to her chest as she took a deep breath. "I'll be right back with something to drink. Don't move."

She bustled back into the restaurant as I stared at my hands. I didn't know what had come over me. Before long, she was back, carrying a tray with two glasses and two bowls. One small, one large. She put the larger bowl on the patio for Finn and slid the small one over to Briar's chair. The two glasses of what looked like lemonade followed. Her sweet gesture was just part of the reason she was my best friend.

"Thanks, Meggie. You're the best," I said, taking a sip and confirming it was indeed her special lemonade. "Oh, that's good. What did you add this time?"

"Fresh lavender from the pots over there," she said, pointing to her left. "It's finally grown enough I can harvest some. Now, tell me what's wrong."

I didn't know where to start, but suddenly, everything came pouring out of me, the words nearly falling over each other in their mad rush to get out of my head. I didn't even think about how she'd react to the news that I could talk to my pets. I knew her well enough to know she'd be as thrilled as I was. By the time I got to my vision and what we'd discovered on the trail, she went pale again.

I took another sip of lemonade, my straw making a sucking sound as I hit the bottom of the glass. Meggie made a move to stand, and I put a hand on hers to keep her in place.

"It's fine. I don't need a refill."

"I might," she said, shooting me a smile as she finished her glass and leaned back in her chair, looking at Finn. "Wow. That's a lot to unpack there, Tess. I don't know where to start. Why didn't you call me last night? Or this morning before you hared off to find a body by yourself?"

I grimaced and dragged a finger through the ring of moisture from the glass left on the wooden table top.

"I wasn't thinking. Honestly, I didn't expect to find a body. I was really thinking it was just an awful dream. Then, when I found her..."

She took my hand and squeezed it.

"That must have been terrible. I'm so sorry you had to go through all of that. Did Jace say... Do they know who she was?"

I shook my head.

"No. He called her a Jane Doe. It's terrible, Meggie. That poor woman. I felt her fear. Her terror. She deserves to have justice. She has a name. I just need to find out who she is. Maybe if I do, I'll learn who the killer is."

"You said she had red, curly hair?"

"Yep. It was curlier than yours. All corkscrew type curls. She would have been distinctive. I wish I'd gotten a look at her face."

"Maybe it's best that you didn't. I can't say I've seen anyone with that description around here. You know how I am when I see one of my curly girls. I always want their routine."

Her hands drifted up to the cloud of hair corralled in a pony tail and I smiled. Meggie didn't know just how much I envied her beautiful hair. It always looked amazing. Well, except maybe right after she got up.

"Could you ask around? You know so many people… I know you've got a lot going on, though."

"Of course! You know, I could ask Jay. He's got that bar downtown. He sees all kinds of people. We've got our weekly meeting tomorrow for all the vendors. It will be the perfect time to ask. And I might ask some locals who come in here, too, until then. We'll find out who she is, Tessa."

My shoulders relaxed. If Meggie said she was going to do something, she did it. With her help, the odds of finding out the woman's identity just went up by leaps and bounds. I squeezed her hand.

"Can I help you get ready for the day? I've already taken up a bunch of your prep time."

She glanced at her watch and shot upward.

"Oh shoot. If you wouldn't mind? I need to get all these tables cleaned and get some stuff ready in the kitchen. I've got Kevin back there doing prep, but he might need a hand."

"Say no more. I'll get the cleaner and rag and pitch in."

Meggie beamed and headed inside. I followed on her heels and grabbed the cleaning supplies from the cabinet where she stored them and headed back to join Finn and Briar. Cleaning the tables was a great mindless activity that let my brain mull over what had happened while my hands kept busy.

I was almost done by the time Meggie came back out. She had another bottle of cleaner in hand and a rag, but she grinned as she saw me cleaning the last one.

"I may need to keep you on full time. Thanks, Tess. I appreciate you pitching in."

"Least I could do, since I'm the one who's been yapping half the morning. Oh, don't let me forget, Paul wanted a green chile burger to go. Maybe by the time I get back over there, he'll have the house opened up."

Meggie glanced at her feet and twisted the rag between her hands.

"It sounds incredible. Maybe I can come by and look at it some time?"

"Of course! I'll ask Paul to give you the grand tour. You won't believe it, Meg. It's such a gorgeous house. Not at all what I was expecting. It will be perfect for Paul. I'd love to live there, but I need room for these guys to run around."

"Speaking of that, we kind of glossed over the whole talking to them thing, what with the discovery of a body. Are you serious? You can really talk to them?"

I beamed as I finished wiping up the last table. Finn and Briar were sitting in the sun on the patio, their legs stretched out as they whispered together. What I had always taken for the two of them enjoying each other's company was way more intense than I'd realized. They were just as good of friends as Meggie and I were.

"No joke, Megs. They're hilarious. Briar is so... snarky? That's the word. But not meanly. In a fun way."

"I heard that," Briar said, swiveling one pointed ear in my direction.

"I wasn't whispering," I said, winking at Meggie.

She giggled and shook her head, tucking the rag into the pocket of her apron.

"How cool is this, though? I remember when we were kids, and you were convinced you could talk to all the woodland creatures. You got your wish."

Only Meggie could say something like that without a single shred of jealousy rearing its head. Her eyes were full of wonder as she looked at my pets. She turned to face me and surprised me by squeezing me into a tight hug.

"I'm just so happy for you. And Paul. If anyone deserves gifts like that, it's you two."

She meant it. That was clear. I squeezed her back and felt my emotions rushing to the surface again. I sniffed hard and stepped back.

"You're the actual gift, Meggie. I'd better let you finish getting prepped. I already hear cars pulling out up front."

She nodded and looked at her watch again.

"It's about that time. I'll go tell Kevin to whip up some burgers for you. I'll toss in a few treats for these guys."

She stopped to pet them as she walked by on the patio. Finn

whisked her tail around, tongue lolling as Meggie scratched her head. Briar was a bit more dignified, but only a little. I called them over and we retreated to the farthest table to wait for our order.

"What now?" Briar asked before yawning widely, the back of her pink throat showing.

"I guess we'll deliver Paul's lunch and see if the locksmith has come by. I'd love to see the inside of that house. After that? Probably swing by the office and then head home. I don't know about you guys, but that early start this morning is catching up with me."

Finn put her head on my shoe and sighed.

"Me too. I could use a nap. This sun feels so nice."

Briar stretched out on the table top, her black coat gleaming in the sunshine, as she nodded off. I breathed in a centering sigh and looked around the peaceful patio. Meggie had done a wonderful job furnishing it to reflect her personality. Flower pots were everywhere, and at night, she'd flip on the fairy lights that made the place positively magical.

I smiled slightly at that thought. Who would've ever guessed I'd inherit magic? I just wished I knew more about the woman who'd left it to us. Who was Euphemia Hawthorne? I pulled out my phone while I waited for my food and did a quick search on her name, not expecting to see much. A few results popped up, but nothing that seemed to be relevant. I sighed and put my phone away. Maybe we'd learn more about her inside her house.

Meggie came out, carrying a bag loaded with takeout containers, and my stomach gave an appreciative rumble as I took it from her.

"Thanks, Meg. What do I owe you?"

"Meh. I'll put it on your tab."

"Meggie..."

"Nope. Not listening. Gotta go. Stay safe, Tessa. I worry about you going out there on your hikes with someone out there prowling around."

"I'll be fine. At least I'll be with a group of people. And I've got the two best bodyguards anyone could ask for."

Finn lifted her head and wagged her tail while Briar stood, stretching so hard she made the table vibrate underneath her.

"Well, when you put it like that. You guys watch over her, okay?"

Finn woofed softly, making Meggie smile as she leaned down to ruffle her fur.

"We'll be fine. You be careful, too, okay? Let me know what you hear from Jay and the gang at your meeting."

A loud clanging sound came from the kitchen and Meggie's feet automatically moved in that direction.

"Go. We'll talk later."

She scurried in, waving as we headed off the patio. The smells coming from the takeout bag filled the Land Rover and Finn never took her eyes off the bag as I stowed it in the backseat next to Briar.

"Let's go see if the locksmith showed up yet and then we can have some lunch."

I reversed out of my spot and headed for Paul's new house, still amazed at all the massive changes that had taken place in the past twenty-four hours, while part of me wondered what else was on the horizon that might shake everything up even more.

Chapter Twelve

Paul's truck was still parked in front of the house when we got back, but he was nowhere to be found. Once I found a spot to park, this time, much closer to the house, I got Finn and Briar unloaded, with a few grumbles from the increasingly hungry cat. I grabbed the bag of food and hoped it was still hot.

As I walked up the driveway, I noticed the door was standing wide open and my heart rate ratcheted up a little. This was it. I was going to see what was inside, and more importantly, hopefully learn more about Euphemia Hawthorne. I poked my head inside and hollered for Paul.

"Come on in," came his answering shout, from somewhere deep in the house. "I hope you brought food. I'm famished."

"Yeah, yeah."

I closed the door behind me and unclipped Finn and Briar's leads. The cat headed directly for the back of the house, almost as if she'd been here before, while my border collie hung close, her side never too far from my leg. Her nose was down, scouring the polished wood floors that looked as though they had to be nearly one hundred years old, and still in incredible condition.

The house was hushed, almost weirdly so, as I trailed after Briar, my gaze snagging every few feet on a new wonder. Whether it was a unique painting on the wall, an intricate piece of glass work on a shelf, or the stained glass window that dominated the kitchen, by the time I found Briar, my mouth was hanging open in awe.

"This place is..."

I looked at Briar and waited for her to finish. Instead, she shook her head and shrugged her little shoulders.

"There aren't any words."

I nodded my agreement, feeling much the same. A small wooden table sat off the kitchen, looking out towards a fenced in back yard. I smiled to see it, envisioning many nights in the future when I'd bring Finn and Briar to visit their uncle Paul, and they could romp around in the backyard, and I wouldn't worry about them wandering into traffic here in town. Not that they would, but I still felt overprotective, even now.

Footsteps sounded behind me, and Paul popped around the corner. His dark blond hair was disheveled, but he looked triumphant as our eyes met. The brown depths, flecked with green, much like my own eyes, said more than words ever could. I simply nodded.

"I know, right? I've only just walked from the front door into here and I'm already astonished."

"You haven't even seen the best part."

I cocked my head to the side and waited.

"And that would be?"

"Food first. I can barely think I'm so hungry. My gosh, that smells delicious," he said, taking the bag out of my hand and inhaling. "Let's grab some plates and we can eat at the table."

I narrowed my eyes, but I knew my brother well enough to know I'd get nothing out of him until he ate. Whatever treasure he'd found, I'd just have to wait. Ugh.

He poked around the cupboards until he found the one with plates stacked inside. He passed over two and I raised an eyebrow, still holding out my hand.

"What?"

"Finn and Briar are hungry, too."

"Oh. You feed them on plates?"

"Well, I didn't bring in their travel bowls from the car, and this is a celebration, after all. So, grab some extra plates. If it makes you queasy, I can wash them for you."

He glanced around the room, grinning when he spotted the dishwasher in the corner.

"No need. Look at that! Finally, a dishwasher."

I heaved a sigh that bordered on envious, but honestly, I really didn't need one. My tiny kitchen wouldn't even hold a portable unit, and it took little enough time to wash the few dishes I dirtied each day. But I was truly glad for my brother. I carried the plates to the table and Paul was right behind me, already digging into the bag.

"How was Meggie?"

I twisted to see his expression, but it was carefully neutral.

"Good. She's gonna check around with her restaurant buddies and see if anyone saw the woman around town. Luckily enough, they're having their meeting tomorrow, so it shouldn't take long to find out. How long did you have to wait for the locksmith?"

He passed over three boxes and grabbed the one on the bottom with his name scrawled on it. I smiled as I noticed Meggie had put a smiley face in the center of the 'A' in Paul. That, or maybe Kevin had. Who knew? I quickly unboxed the treats for my pets, plating up their non-seasoned burgers and then unboxed mine. Finn gave my plate a deep sniff before focusing on her food. She loved the smell of green chiles, but after one disastrous attempt, a few months ago, when she snuck a bite of my burger, she'd never tried to swipe my food again.

I dipped a fry in the sauce and waited for Paul to answer. His mouth bulged as he tried to chew the giant bite he'd taken.

"Nice, Paul. Holy smokes, you weren't kidding about being starved."

"I skipped breakfast," he finally said, wiping his mouth. "Oh. You asked about the locksmith. He showed up about a half hour after you left. Nice guy. He recommended changing out all the locks on the place. I made an appointment for him to come back later in the week."

"Cool. So, what was this you were saying about something you found here?" I asked, swiveling my head around and taking in the decor.

"Nope. Not telling you. You've got to see it to believe it. This house, Tess... I can't get over it. It's literally like it was built for me."

I swallowed a bite of my burger and looked at him. I couldn't remember the last time I'd seen him this happy.

"Maybe it was. Who knows? I want to learn more about this aunt of ours. She seems like such a cool person. I hope she wasn't lonely. Gosh, I wish we'd known her when she was alive. I have so many questions."

His eyes sparkled with merriment as he finished chewing.

"That's probably why she waited to introduce herself until after she was gone. So you couldn't badger the poor dear."

I tossed a fry in his direction, but disappointingly, he caught it and devoured it. Brothers. I rolled my eyes and vowed not to make that mistake again. Meggie's fries were too good to waste like that.

Briar looked up from her spot on the floor. Her plate was licked clean, and she sniffed delicately, giving me a piteous look.

"Yes, Briar?"

"Well, since you're tossing those fries away, you might as well give me and Finn one. I mean, we've been going since before dawn, without a single nap. A little sustenance would go a long way to supporting your faithful animals."

I raised an eyebrow and swung my gaze over to Finn, who looked as innocent as a border collie could ever look. Who was I kidding? I'd never been able to resist those brown eyes, and I would not start today. I dutifully handed over two fries, breaking Briar's up into small pieces and worked on finishing my lunch.

Paul beat me, and sat, ever impatient, joggling his leg underneath the table as he waited for me to finish. Part of me wanted to slow down and see how long it would take him to crack, but I wanted to see the house and whatever he'd found. I grinned and cleaned up my mess, tucking the wrappers back into the food boxes.

"Finally. I thought you'd never finish. Put the plates on the counter. I'll worry about them later. You've got to see this."

Paul looked like a kid as he hurried down the hall. The rest of us followed at a more stately pace, but excitement jolted through my veins as I came to a halt behind where he stood in the doorway of a room.

"Kinda hard to see around you there, Paul. You make a better wall than a door."

"Hey, I'm building anticipation. Okay, ready?"

He stepped aside and my jaw felt like it hit the floor, rebounded, and fell again as I saw the library in front of me. Every single square inch of wall space was covered with wooden shelving. Two beautifully paned art deco windows let in just the right amount of light, giving the room a soft glow. Two chairs that had to have been built in the 1930s sat, crouching in the middle of the room on a plush rug.

"Look at the sides of the chairs," Paul said, his voice filled with excitement. "I've seen nothing like it before."

I walked into the room and knelt next to the chairs, my knee sinking into the plush carpet. On each side of the chairs, there was a built-in bookcase, just waiting for more books. I turned and smiled at my brother.

"This is so cool. I can't believe it. How many books do you think are in here?"

"Hundreds. Thousands maybe. I'll have to do an inventory. Some of these books are so old I'm scared to touch them. I even spotted a few first editions. This is incredible, Tessa. I can't believe it."

I turned around slowly, taking it all in. Euphemia had never met us, but somehow, she'd known exactly what we'd like. For me, the ability to talk to my pets was a gift I'd treasure for the rest of my life, and pray that I'd never lose it. The nightmare/vision thing was a little iffy, but maybe I'd get used to it. And for Paul, an antique book and this treasure box of a house.

"I wish we could thank her," I said, finally. "I wonder what she was like."

"Well, check out this section," Paul said, gently leading me to the left and stopping in front of a row of books bound in midnight blue. "These are her journals. There's one for every year for the past fifty years. I think you'll find the answers there."

I touched the spines of the journals with a feeling of reverence and pulled out the one on the end, glancing at the cover.

"This is for this year, Paul. Oh, do you mind if I take this home with me?"

"Not at all. You can take anything you want from here. As long as you bring it back, anyway," he said, sticking his tongue out at me. "And don't bend the spines. You know how much I hate that."

I rolled my eyes as I gripped the book to my chest.

"I did that once. I was five."

"Well, still. That was one of my favorite books."

Finn and Briar sniffed around the room, the cat shadowing the dog. Neither one seemed too concerned, so I didn't worry too much about the magical traps Briar mentioned earlier. Maybe she was right, and they were keyed to us since we were family. I gripped the book harder.

"What else have you found?"

"Nothing quite this spectacular. The home's all on one-level, and even though it's obviously old, it's in incredible shape. All the mechanical things are only a few years old, and the roof looks brand new. This is just not what I was expecting. I can't believe it, Tess. I feel almost guilty."

I spun on my heel and looked at my brother.

"Why?"

"Because I got all of this and you got a lightning bug and a wooden box."

"A lightning bug that apparently imparted magical powers, thank you very much. And I love that wooden box. It's so cool. Besides, maybe when it's all said and done, I'll end up a powerful witch and you'll be my faithful sidekick," I said, elbowing him in the side. "Besides, I can talk to Finn and Briar. That's more than anything I could ever ask for."

His eyes searched mine and apparently, what he saw in them settled his emotions. He gave me a sharp nod and his grin came back.

"Come on. You gotta see the furniture in the main bedroom. It's incredible."

I trailed after him, followed closely by Finn and Briar. I had a feeling it wouldn't take Paul long to cancel his lease and move his stuff in here. Heck, I couldn't blame him. This was one incredible house.

"I've got Sunday free if you want help to move your things," I said, hollering down the hallway.

"Sweet. I'll probably just donate all my furniture. It's pretty ratty and I've got everything I need here."

Maybe not everything, but it was certainly better than his current living arrangements. I nodded as I traced the wainscoting that lined the hall. My finger came up free from dust and I rubbed my fingertips together. I don't know how she'd done it, but this place was spotless, even after weeks of being closed up.

By the time Paul was done trotting around the house, showing off his finds, my eyes were getting heavy and my pets had already crashed in the library, cuddling on the plush rug. I gathered them up, and we headed for home, the prized diary still in my hand. I couldn't wait to read it, but something told me that would have to wait until tomorrow, after my scheduled hike. I'd need to be up bright and early to meet everyone at the trailhead.

Chapter Thirteen

The beginning of a hike is always an interesting experience, particularly when you're dealing with a mix of tourists from every corner of the globe. Thanks to the fact I live in Colorado, in the foothills of the Rocky Mountains, the flow of tourists seems to be never-ending. Which, on one hand, is an excellent thing since my business depends on them to survive. Well, But... Let's just say it keeps my life interesting.

I like to arrive early for a hike, taking the time to warm up at the trailhead, and find a moment of peace before everyone else arrives. Thankfully, I'd slept well, curled between Finn and Briar, and no visions had crept into my dreams. They were currently chatting quietly in the back of the Land Rover while I worked out a kink in my calf muscle. My ears perked up as I realized they were discussing the murder.

"I'm just saying we need more information. We should go back to that trailhead and see if we can track anything. Maybe there's some evidence the cops didn't find. You know how Jace is. He couldn't find his way out of a wet paper bag with a guide dog."

"Briar, we both checked the scents while we were there, while the trail was still relatively fresh. We didn't pick up on anything then."

"But what about that strange man we saw? You saw how Jace reacted to that information. I have a feeling about that guy. We need to do more. We can't let him get away with this."

Finn woofed softly and shook her head as I got closer to them.

"I know how you feel, guys. Maybe Meggie will come up with something that will help us find out who the woman was. Until then, we're kind of stuck. I don't want her to remain a Jane Doe. Someone out there is missing her."

"Can Paul run a check on missing persons? He's got access to databases for the paper, doesn't he?"

I blinked at Briar's very perceptive question. I didn't know she understood the inner-workings of human technology so well. A sinking feeling hit my stomach as I realized we'd wasted a day looking up important information, completely distracted by Paul's new home.

"I didn't even think of that. Neither did Paul. Let me text him."

I was tapping on my phone when a camper van rolled into the parking lot. My first hiker had arrived. I tucked my phone away and pushed off the bumper, smiling as the woman got out of her vehicle.

I put her age at around her mid-sixties, and smiled as soon as I spotted her floppy hat, festooned with many pins. Her face was free of makeup, heavily lined, and her blue eyes looked sharp as she sized me up.

"Wild Peak Expeditions, right? I'm Dot Havers. Looks like I'm the first one here, huh?"

I held out my hand for her to shake and her grip was sturdy, even though she looked as though a stiff wind would knock her flat.

"Good morning, Dot. I'm Tessa Windsor. This is Finn, my border collie, and Briar. They'll be coming with us on today's hike."

She grinned, her crow's feet spreading like cracks in dry ground.

"Fabulous. Looks like you've got an adventure cat on your hands. They're such beautiful animals."

She held out a practiced hand for both animals to sniff and my estimation of Dot increased a few points. Now that she was close, I could see the pins on her hat were for a variety of local state parks. She turned to face me and I nodded towards her hat.

"Looks like you're no stranger to hikes."

She unleashed a broad grin and patted her hat.

"Been to every state park in Colorado, Wyoming, and Montana. I'm on my way to New Mexico to the do the same thing. It's part of my bucket list after retirement. California will be next year. Or Utah. I haven't decided yet."

"What brings you to Collinsville?"

"Just passing through. Saw your advertisement in a local cafe when I had breakfast two days ago and stuck around. When you travel with your house, that's easy to do."

I already liked Dot immensely. She might be tiny, but her wiry legs were packed with muscle. I wouldn't have to worry too much about her. She could handle herself, even on a challenging hike like the one I'd planned for today.

Two more vehicles pulled in, and I shaded my eyes as they found their parking spots. Group dynamics on a hike were always interesting. Invariably, you had at least one or two experienced hikers, like Dot, while the rest were typically new to the sport, or just out for a gamble because they wanted to check something off a to-do list.

A man around my age came jogging over, flashing a very white smile as he approached. His muscles had muscles that were all on display thanks to the tight tank-top and bike shorts he was wearing, and he was sporting a hydration pack. His short cropped blond hair revealed his pink scalp as he nodded in my direction.

"Morning. Scott Trager. How much longer until the hike starts? I want to make sure I have time for my warm-up routine."

I glanced at the clipboard I had leaned in the back, next to Finn, and checked my watch.

"We've got two more people scheduled to arrive. We'll give them ten minutes past the start date to show and then we'll head out."

"Sweet. I'll be ready."

He jogged off a short distance and started stretching his hamstrings while he looked towards the mountains in the distance. Dot let out a low whistle.

"Didn't know we'd have eye candy on this hike. I'm glad I signed up."

I couldn't suppress a giggle as the other hiker approached. She was around forty, and her hair was tied back into a tight ponytail. Between her sensible outfit and the fact her hiking boots weren't new, I guessed she was used to hiking. So far, three out of the five seemed to be seasoned, making my job that much easier.

"Hi," the woman said, with a shy head bob. "Frances Whiting. I hope I didn't make you wait."

"Not at all Frances. We've got two more people scheduled and we'll be ready to head out. This is Dot, and my two companions who'll be hiking with us."

She greeted Dot, and then her face lit up when she spotted Finn and Briar. Finn's tail wagged gently as Frances approached them.

"Oh, how wonderful is this? The cat likes to hike too? I've never seen a cat who could do something like that."

Briar's green eyes narrowed as she shot me a look and I smothered my smile.

"She loves it. Not all cats do, but she lives for the outdoors."

A muscle car careened into the lot, engine revving, and I straightened, placing myself in front of the back of my vehicle, moving Dot and Frances behind me. The driver parked across three spaces and I let out a sigh. I knew it was too good to be true that everyone in this group was going to be fun.

A man and a woman got out and the first thing I noticed was their footwear. The woman was wearing sandals with thin leather straps, more appropriate for the beach than the wilderness, and the man was wearing flat street-style tennis shoes with no laces. Oh boy.

I pasted on a practiced smile as they approached. They were in their early twenties, and from the way they were hanging on each other, I guessed they were newly in a relationship.

"Hey," the man said, pushing his floppy brown hair out of his eyes. "I'm Jayden, and this is Tiffany. Hope we're not late."

Tiffany waggled her fingers and giggled, tossing her long blonde hair over her shoulder as she looked around, zeroing in on a point behind me. Her mouth fell slightly open as Jayden tensed next to her. I pivoted and saw Scott performing a set of deep squats that, thanks to his skintight shorts, outlined every muscle on his backside. I quickly turned away as Dot elbowed Frances.

"Nice to meet you both. Tiffany, do you have another pair of shoes with you? This hike has some pretty serious sections with loose scree. I don't want you to get hurt. Same for you, Jayden. I don't think those shoes are going to hold up."

"I'll be fine," Tiffany said, tearing her eyes from Scott's backside with visible effort. "I wear these everywhere."

I suppressed a sigh, already making plans to cut this hike short, while Dot muttered behind me. Tiffany gasped, pulling my attention back to her.

"Oh, look at the cute little doggie. Oh my goodness, is that a widdle pussy cat? She's soooooo cute."

She moved towards the Land Rover, and Briar's expression had me quickly moving to block her access. If there were two things Briar didn't tolerate, it was fawning attention and baby talk. Yep, this hike was definitely going to be interesting.

Finn vaulted out of the back of the Land Rover, whirled around and waited for me to latch her leash while Briar took her time getting down, stretching deeply, much to Tiffany's delight.

"Oh, she's coming with us? This is so cool!"

Dot flinched at the loud squealing noise coming from Tiffany and elbowed Frances in the side.

"Lets take the lead, Frannie."

Frances let the older woman pull her towards the beginning of the trail as I rounded everyone else up. Scott jogged in place, got in a few more hamstring stretches, and sprinted down the trail, rounding the two older women. Oh boy.

I clipped on Briar's lead and headed out, trying to center myself in nature, as I always did at the start of the hike. Focus on the blue sky, the slight breeze, and the feeling of the sun on my cheeks. I was blessed to work outside, doing what I love. I repeated that mantra a few times as we made our way down the trail, slowly overtaking the hikers until I was in the lead. Well, almost in the lead. I spotted Scott's hydration pack a few yards down the trail, but I wasn't about to go haring off to overtake him.

"Did you hear about the murder?" Frances asked Dot as the two women walked side-by-side on the dirt path.

"What? No. Although, I suppose it's everywhere. Even nice places like this. What happened?"

I slowed my steps, listening in.

"Well, I heard a woman got butchered on a hiking trail on the other side of town. I guess it was just gruesome," Tiffany piped up, her pale face flushed as she struggled to keep up with us.

"Yeah, we almost didn't come, but I told babes I'd protect her no matter what," Jayden said, beaming at Tiffany. "Ain't nothing or no one gonna harm my baby."

She leaned against him, pressing a kiss to his cheek before turning back to Frances and Dot, who'd stopped in shock at Tiffany's description of the murder.

"Butchered?" Dot said, her hand creeping up towards her neck. "That sounds awful. Where was this?"

I needed to step in, even though I didn't want to.

"It happened on Ridgeline Trail," I said, as Finn whined softly. "She wasn't butchered. She was strangled. They're looking for her killer. The police believe it was a personal attack, not something random. In a group like this, we're perfectly safe."

Hopefully, that was true. Frances's brown eyes were enormous as she looked at me.

"How do you know all this?"

I wasn't about to admit that I was the one who'd found her, or that I'd had an eerie vision before her death.

"I know a deputy on the sheriff's force."

"What's going on?"

I turned to see Scott had rejoined us, hands on hips, while he looked at us. I opened my mouth to answer, but Tiffany beat me to it.

"We were talking about the killing on a hiking trail near here. It's just terrible. I can't imagine what would drive someone to do something so horrible."

"I wouldn't worry about it too much," Scott said, shrugging. "It's broad daylight and I don't think anyone's gonna go against me. I'll keep you safe."

He flexed both arms, showing off his biceps, and Jayden's face went an ugly color of red. I rolled my eyes and strode ahead. I had to get control of this situation and the group before it spiraled out of control.

"Alright, everyone, that's enough of that. The cops are working on it. Now, this hike is known for its wide variety of rock formations and interesting plants. If you'll fall in behind me, Scott, I'll lead the way."

His eyebrows went up, but he bobbed his head, letting me pass as I steered Finn around him. Briar trotted along, her long fur rippling in the breeze as we took the lead. Luckily, Frances struck up a conversation with Dot about the pins on her hat, leaving Jayden and Tiffany to bring up the rear alone. I had a feeling I'd be checking on them often, but for now, I just wanted to get the hike officially started.

For about an hour, everything went smoothly. I went through my spiel about the historical facts of the trail, focusing on my particular interest in plants, thanks to my degree in botany. Everyone got along, and no more discussions about the murder threatened to spoil the beautiful day.

When we reached the last section of the trail, with the scree, I slowed everyone down and looked at Tiffany. Her feet were already scratched, and I was pretty sure she had some massive blisters from the way she kept wincing with every step. My shoulders sank.

"Okay, everyone. This is the difficult section of the trail. Tiffany, how are you holding up? You look a little sore."

Her face was bright red as she backhanded the sweat from her forehead. Jayden didn't look like he was in much better shape.

"I don't know if I can keep going. That looks really steep. Can we turn back?"

Dot groaned and put her hands on her scrawny hips.

"Look, you were told about having the right gear. The rest of us paid good money to go on the full hike. It's not fair."

Frances nodded, but kept glancing between everyone's faces. Scott smiled and walked closer to Tiffany.

"You could take a break here and wait for everyone to finish. It's not much further. Is it Miss Windsor?"

I shook my head.

"About fifteen more minutes before we turn back."

"Alright. Tell you what, I can hang out with you so you won't be alone," Scott said, grinning broadly. "I've already hit my target for my heart rate, so I don't mind."

Jayden's eyes went to slits as he shook his head.

"I'll stay. Go on ahead."

"Suit yourself," Scott said with a shrug. "Just trying to be polite."

I didn't like leaving people behind, but I could see there was no way Tiffany could keep going. Briar heaved a sigh and sidled close, speaking so softly I could barely hear her.

"I'll stay with them and keep them safe. Finn will know if I need anything."

I was tempted to reply, but I knew there was no way of hiding my much louder voice. Instead, I looked at her, hoping she'd be able to read my mind. The thought of leaving her with people I didn't know didn't sit well with me.

"It's fine. But you owe me one. I want some salmon when we get home. I can already tell she's going to mess up my fur."

I bit my lip to keep a laugh from burbling up and nodded instead. Briar walked towards Tiffany, tail held high, and stopped in front of her feet.

"Oh, the kitty wants to stay with us. How sweet is that? Come here, little kitty. Let me pet you."

It only took one look at Briar to know that the salmon order just got doubled as Tiffany reached for the cat, squishing her to her chest. Jayden breathed out a sigh of what had to be relief as he sunk down on a nearby boulder.

"All right. We'll be back in about thirty minutes. Stay right here, okay?"

"Sure thing. I'm too tired to walk anywhere else," Jayden said, pushing his hair out of his eyes.

The time flew by as I led the rest of the group up the steep section. Frances slipped, but Scott steadied her with a grin, making the poor woman blush so red she resembled a walking tomato. We crested the top of the section that marked the end of the hike, and Dot turned, surveying the landscape.

"I'm glad I came. Even with those two yahoos. This was all worth it."

I couldn't disagree as I looked across the valley below. This was one of my favorite trails, simply because of this view. I let everyone catch their breath before heading back down, Finn close at my heels. She'd been antsy since we'd left Briar behind, and I felt the same way. Luckily, the way down was always faster, and before we knew it, we spotted Tiffany and Jayden, right where we'd left them. Briar was lounging on the top of the boulder, looking more annoyed than usual.

"Feeling better?" I asked Tiffany, as I scooped Briar up into a hug.

"Much," Tiffany said, but she still winced when she stood.

"All right, let's head back to the trailhead. Does anyone have questions about the area and the hike?"

"Is it pretty common to have murders on these trails?" Jayden asked as he pushed to his feet and fell in at the back of the group. "I mean, it's way out in the wilderness. It's a perfect place to murder someone."

A chill went down my spine at his matter-of-fact tone, and I turned to look at him.

"Not at all. Our little area is very peaceful."

"Huh. Strange."

He didn't elaborate, and there was no way I wanted to keep that line of conversation going. Instead, I defaulted into a quick history lesson of the pioneers who'd forged some of these trails, and by the time we made it back to the trailhead, blessedly, no one else brought up the murder.

Dot gave me a surprise hug once we reached our vehicles, and I hugged her back, making sure I didn't squeeze her bony shoulders too hard.

"It was a pleasure meeting you," she said as she stepped back. "Best hike I've ever had. You have so much knowledge. If I'm ever in the area again, I'll book another one."

Frances murmured a thank you and headed for her vehicle, escorted by Scott. Tiffany and Jayden limped towards their car without a backwards glance, and as soon as they were inside, he revved the engine and pealed out of the lot. I had a feeling they would not be repeat customers.

Once everyone was gone, I opened up the back of the Land Rover and Finn hopped in, panting as I pulled out her collapsible water bowl and filled it. The temperature had definitely risen, and I was glad we'd finished the hike when we had.

"Look. Tess! Look over there!"

I whipped my head around at Briar's whispered command and immediately spotted a man standing in the trees, staring at us. My heart stuttered as Finn growled low in her chest, the sound menacing.

I shifted my pack to my side, hand on the zipper, hoping I wouldn't need the gun hidden inside of it. My fingers shook as they hovered.

Finn launched out of the back of the vehicle, barking like mad, and the man moved off, melting into the trees. As he turned, I spotted a familiar backpack, the blue and green Navajo pattern flashing through the brush as he disappeared.

Briar joined Finn, every bit of her body tense as they faced the woods, never taking their eyes off the treeline.

Chapter Fourteen

Several seconds passed, but they felt like hours as I strained my eyes, half-hoping to glimpse the strange man in the woods, and mostly dreading that I would. Finn's hackles were completely up, and Briar was fluffed up so much she looked like a black and white bobcat, ready to take on anything.

I forced myself to take a breath. And another one. Slowly, I relaxed, dropping my hand. Whoever that man was, he was gone. Finn woofed out one more low bark and slunk back to my side, tail held low.

"Okay. So that was weird, right?"

"Uh, yeah," Briar said, shooting me a look. "That's the second time we've seen him. Once you could write off as a coincidence. Twice? And in two different locations? Nope. He's tracking you, Tessa. I don't like it."

"I couldn't get a scent of him," Finn said, hanging her head miserably as she leaned against my side. "I could only smell deer."

"But there aren't many deer in this area," Briar said, scanning the woods with her sharp green eyes. "Hmmm."

I shifted in place and stroked Finn's head, hoping to lift her out of her funk. I always knew these two were protective, but hearing it from their mouths brought home how much they cared for me.

"We should probably call Jace, huh?" I said, already knowing the answer.

"*You* should call Jace. We want nothing to do with him," Briar said, leaping into the back of the Land Rover. "We really need to develop better connections in law enforcement. It's too bad we're out of the jurisdiction of the town. Maybe the police would have better members. Ben used to be a cop. And you could tell he was a darn good one."

Ben Walsh was Hannah Murphy's boyfriend, and we'd met him during that awful hike with the Prescotts. Calm under pressure, quick to take charge, and knew exactly what to do in a dangerous situation. Right now, I could use a good head like that. Unfortunately, he was a hundred miles away, and no longer in law enforcement. If this case dragged on, though, I was strongly considering calling him.

"Well, unfortunately, this is in the county, so Jace is our best bet."

Briar muttered something that sounded a lot like he was *my* best bet, while they'd reserve the option to pick someone else. But I ignored her as I dug my phone out of my pocket. I'd saved Jace's direct line in my phone, even though I never used it. Today, I was glad I had it. I punched the call button and waited while I leaned against my vehicle. Finn's eyes never left the trees as the phone rang.

"Well, if it isn't Tessa. I didn't expect to hear from you, well, ever. And if this is about the woman you found yesterday, I can't tell you anything. We're still trying to find out her identity. And you can let your brother know that, too, since you tell him everything."

I bit back several choice comments that sprang to mind. Irritating Jace would not be in my favor. Not today anyway.

"Hello to you, too, Jace. Look, I hate to bother you, but something strange just happened and I... Well, I need to report it."

Silence hung in the cell phone lines between us and I squinched up my eyes, hating the fact that I had to deal with him.

"What happened, Tess?"

I sighed. Now I was talking to official Jace Roberts, the deputy. Not the ex-boyfriend.

"You know that guy I mentioned yesterday? The one I saw in the parking lot at the trailhead. I just saw him again. But I'm at Pine Loop, doing a hike with a group."

"Did they see him as well?"

My shoulders slumped as I looked at my hiking boots, toeing off a bit of mud that stuck to the toe.

"No. They'd all left. I was just packing up when I spotted him in the treeline. He was just staring at me, Jace. It was weird."

"You're certain it was the same man?"

"Well, I never saw his face. He was too far away. But he had that same pack on. I'm sure of it."

"So he didn't approach you?"

"No... He just stared for a while and then moved off through the trees. I don't know how long he was standing there, though. It really bothered my pets."

He let out a long sigh and I could envision him shaking his head at me through the phone.

"Tess, you know there's no crime in hiking and looking at people. He was probably just curious about what you were up to. Maybe he recognized you from yesterday and thought it was odd to see you again. Unless he threatened you, there's not much I can do."

His words fell like little lead balloons, squashing any hope I'd had that he would take me seriously.

"But, it's odd. Don't you think?"

"Free country, Tessa. Now, if you'll excuse me, I need to get back to this case. We've got no leads to speak of."

"I just gave you a lead! What if this is the guy who killed that woman? What if he's after me now?"

"Now, Tessa. Let's not get hysterical. Tell you what, you see him again, you let me know and I'll see if I can get a unit to cruise up to where you're at. Until then, I'm sorry, but there's nothing I can do."

He ended the call, leaving me staring at my phone, steaming

mad. I ground my teeth together as I put my phone back in my pocket.

"So much for law enforcement," Briar said, her whiskers bristling. "Looks like we're gonna have to take care of this ourselves."

Finn shot me a look filled with worry. I knew Jace had a point. There wasn't a crime in showing up where I was twice, but something bothered me about the whole thing.

"He already knows who you are," Finn said, her voice soft. "Your vehicle has the company name right on it, big as anything."

"She's right, Tessa. All the guy has to do is go to your website and he'll see where you have your next hike scheduled. You're a sitting duck. We all are."

I didn't like the fear that crammed down my throat at her words, but she was right. I also had another hike scheduled for tomorrow, and of course, its location was broadcasted to anyone who wanted to know. Regardless of their intentions. I took a shaky breath.

"Well, that's not concerning or anything."

"We need to investigate this case on our own," Briar said, sitting up tall, her pointy ears held rigid. "Who was the woman who died? Did Paul get back to you?"

I shook my head. When I'd called Jace, I saw I had no new text messages or missed calls. Finn hopped in next to Briar.

"Well, we need to go talk to him. Let's go. Briar was right. Maybe the woman's on a missing person's list and we can find her that way."

"But Jace would have access to the same lists. Probably more. Wouldn't he have already found her?"

"You're asking us to trust Jace to tell you anything? Or do the legwork?" Briar scoffed. "Nope. We do this our way."

She had a point. As usual. I nodded and slung my pack off my shoulder to stow it in the back.

"All right. Let's go to the newspaper office. He's probably busy with a story, and that's why he didn't get back to me."

I closed the back gate of the Land Rover and hopped in, more than ready to get out of the area. I doubted the man was still hanging around, but I couldn't be certain. Getting into town, where I'd be surrounded by people, seemed like a good idea.

It was just before lunchtime by the time I rolled into Collinsville. I turned to go down the street to the newspaper office and my phone rang. My old rig didn't have any fancy bluetooth abilities, so I pulled onto a side street and parked. I couldn't help but smile when I saw Meggie's name on my screen.

"Morning, Meggie. Or I should say afternoon. How was your meeting? I was just heading to talk to Paul."

"I'll meet you there. Kevin can handle opening up today. I've got something, Tess. Jay remembered seeing her. I'm on my way now."

Anticipation rocketed through my core as I nodded.

"Okay. See you in five minutes."

I ended the call and pulled back onto the road while Briar vaulted into the front seat, little cat hairs flying around as she landed gracefully.

"What did Meggie say?"

"She found someone who saw the woman before she died. Meggie's gonna meet us at the newspaper."

Finn let out a sharp bark of happiness that made my ears ring, but I couldn't help but smile as I found a place to park in front of the office. I got their leads clipped back on, knowing full well they wouldn't tolerate being left out of this conversation. Besides, Paul never minded me bringing them inside. As long as Briar stayed off the print equipment. Which she did. Usually, anyway.

"All right, guys. We beat Meggie. Let's head in and wait for her."

I shepherded them inside the building and waved at Connie behind the front desk. She'd worked there for years, even before Paul bought the business, managing both customer service and the classified section. Her brown curly hair sat on her head like a helmet and I knew for a fact she used enough hairspray to keep those curls safe in a storm.

"Hi Connie. Paul in his office?"

"Yep. He's been wrestling with the layout all morning. Go on back. Hi, you two."

She waggled her fingers at Finn and Briar as I led them back to the tiny office where Paul was holed up. An enormous sneeze nearly rattled the door. I rapped on it, but didn't wait for him to answer, turning the knob and rushing in. He looked up from his computer screen, eyes wide.

"Uh, hi. What are you three doing here?"

"Bless you. Did you get my text?"

His eyes strayed to the phone on the other side of his desk and he shook his head. He reached for a tissue and blew his nose.

"Sorry, I've been so focused I didn't even hear the notification. What's up? Everything okay?"

I sat in the chair opposite his desk and patted my lap. Briar flew into it, digging her claws into my leg as she turned around to get comfortable. Finn arranged herself at my feet like she always did.

"We saw that man again. At the Pine Loop trail. I'd just gotten done with my hiking group."

Paul finally looked at me. Really looked at me, and his eyebrows pulled down in a fierce frown.

"Are you okay? What happened?"

"He just stared from the treeline. Briar's the one who spotted him and warned me. Finn went ballistic, and the guy eventually left. But that's not all. Meggie found someone who saw the woman before she died. She's gonna meet us here."

Paul's eyes brightened before he mastered his expression, but I spotted the joy in there before he could mask it. He nodded and clicked around on his computer.

"There. Saved. You're sure it was the same man?"

"Oh, not you too. Jace already gave me the talk about that. Yes, I'm sure."

Paul held up his hands and leaned back in his chair.

"Sorry. That came out wrong. Did you run into Jace?"

I grimaced and shook my head.

"No. I called him. He blew me off about seeing the guy. Said it was a free country and there's nothing he can do about it."

"Well, there's something I can do about it," Paul said, eyes narrowing. "You've got a hike tomorrow, right? I can go with you."

"Paul, you've got the paper to run. You can't babysit me. And think about your allergies. You'll be miserable. Besides, I'll be fine. I've got my gun, and I've got these guys. If I see him again, I might just march over and ask who the heck he is and what he's doing."

Brave words I didn't feel, but it was nice to say them. Paul opened his mouth, his expression clear that I was about to get blasted, but a knock on the door silenced him.

"Come on in."

Meggie's curly head popped in and she smiled when she spotted me.

"Oh good, you're already here. Hi, Paul."

She dimpled at him and immediately dropped her eyes. She took the chair next to me and fussed over Finn, not quite looking at Paul.

"Hi Megs," Paul said. "Tessa said you found someone who knew the woman?"

She nodded, curls bouncing, and glanced at me.

"Jay said a woman matching that description came into his bar three nights ago. He remembered her wild hair. He didn't talk to her, but one of his bartenders did. He said her name was Felicity. She was from Wyoming, on vacation here, but said little. The bouncer saw her later and said she left with a man he didn't recognize. He said the guy was tall and muscular. He wasn't sure if they knew each other, or had just met, but they left together and she was smiling."

She ran out of breath and put a hand to her chest.

"Whew. I wanted to make sure I remembered, so I came right here. Does this help?"

I nodded and met Paul's eyes.

"Can you pull up the missing person's database? Briar suggested you might have access. That's what I texted you about earlier. But now we've got a first name and a state. That's gotta help, right?"

Paul nodded and his fingers flew across the keys.

"Great work, Megs. Let's see if we can find anything. It might take a few minutes to run a full search. I hate to admit it, but there are so many missing people out there and it takes a while to sort through them all. I'll put in her physical appearance, too, in case she wasn't being truthful about her name."

Meggie's eyes shone as she listened and nodded.

"Oh, I hope you find her. That was a great idea, Briar."

My cat preened while we waited for the search results. It felt like we were finally getting somewhere.

Chapter Fifteen

The silence that filled the room while we waited for the search results felt oddly strained and awkward. My fingers sought, and found, Finn's reassuring presence at my feet as Briar shifted in my lap. Meggie flashed me a tight smile, and I searched my inconveniently blank mind to come up with something to say.

"So, how's the restaurant business doing? Everybody pretty happy at the meeting?"

Not a great first attempt, but it was better than stewing in silence. Meggie's eyebrows furrowed, but she nodded.

"Good. It's been a busy tourist season so far, so all the owners are pretty happy. We're working together on bringing some food-centered events together before the end of Fall. Maybe a festival? We're still working out the details and how everything would come together."

"That sounds like fun. Paul, maybe you could interview Meggie and the other owners and do a few pieces to promote it?"

Meggie flashed me a look that promised later retribution, but I pretended to ignore it as Paul raised his head behind his computer screen and gave a hearty sneeze.

"Sorry. Sure. Anything to help, Megs. I think I've got something here, guys."

I inched forward, and Briar put her claws out to steady herself. I automatically untangled them from my shorts as I waited for Paul to continue.

"And? You found her?"

"Well, I think so. The first name doesn't match up, but the middle one does. It might be a long shot, but look. They've got her picture there."

He swiveled the monitor towards me, and I leaned forward a little more. Meggie did too, her soft curls brushing my shoulder. I frowned as I read aloud from the screen.

"Sarah Felicity Greenville. Age, twenty-two. Oh, she's so young. The hair, well, it's hard to tell, but it looks similar. It says she was last seen in Riverton, Wyoming, so that matches up with what Meggie said. I think this might be her, Paul."

Sadness crept through me as I looked at the woman's face on the screen. She didn't look happy in the picture and I couldn't help but wonder about her life. How she'd ended up here, dead at the hands of a madman.

"Riverton? That's on the Wind River reservation, right?" Meggie asked. "We drove through there once when we took that trip to Jackson, Tess. You remember?"

I did. The area was wildly rugged and inhospitable, but had its own peculiar beauty that had stuck with me. It also wasn't that far away.

"I remember. It matches up, Paul. We've got to do something. This could be her. I can't imagine what her family is feeling right now."

Paul nodded as he turned the screen back around.

"We've got an eyewitness who saw her at the bar. I think you're right, Tess. You need to call Jace."

I shook my head and scooted back in my chair, gripping Briar.

"No. I just talked to him. He won't appreciate another call. This one needs to come from you, Paul."

"I could call him…" Meggie offered, but it was clear her heart wasn't in it. "I mean, I'm the one who talked to Jay and his team."

"I'll do it," Paul said, grimacing. "Better do it right now. What's his number, Tess?"

I pulled my phone out and recited Jace's number while Paul punched it in on the desk phone. He ran his hands through his hair, standing it on end while he waited for Jace to answer. It didn't take long for Jace's voice to sound. Paul punched the speakerphone button and sat back in his chair.

"Jace? This is Paul Windsor with the Clarion. I've got some information that I think might be useful in your investigation into the murder that took place on the Ridgeline Trail."

My brother was using his all business voice, and I marveled at how well it worked on Jace. Instead of his usual good-old-boy routine, Jace was all business as he responded.

"All right. What have you got?"

"A woman by the name of Sarah Felicity Greenville, age twenty-two, recently missing from Riverton, Wyoming. Her name matches with a description from a local bar owner who spotted her the day before she died, leaving his bar with an unknown man. The woman pictured has red curly hair, which I believe matches the body you found."

Silence followed while the three of us waited to see what Jace would say. As much as I didn't like the man, he wasn't a corrupt cop. Well, deputy. Just stubborn and irritating. I supposed those traits were useful in his job, but I couldn't help but wish he was different. That we'd never dated.

"I see. Send me the link and I'll look at it. Which bar?"

Paul quickly tapped the speakerphone button, turning it off, as Meggie softly answered.

"The Tap and Forge."

Paul repeated the information for Jace and turned the speakerphone back on.

"Jay's the owner. His bartender saw the woman, and the bouncer saw her leave with a man."

"How did you get this information?"

"I've got my sources. Let me know when you've got it confirmed."

Jace snorted loudly, and I frowned, picturing the look on his face.

"Yeah. Thanks, Windsor."

A dial tone sounded before Paul hung up the phone and smiled at us.

"Well, it's something. Good work, you two. That will make it easier to find her killer."

"But the bouncer didn't know the man," Meggie said, her eyes filled with sadness. "We may know her name, but we're not that much closer to finding out who killed her."

"It will come. At least Jace has somewhere to start."

"And the woman, if we're right, won't be a Jane Doe any more," I said. "That matters. Maybe someone else saw something. If you put it in the paper, maybe someone will come forward. We're on the right track, at least."

"I'm still going with you tomorrow," Paul said, eyes narrowed. "I'll make time, Tess. So don't even try to wiggle out of it."

"What's going on?" Meggie asked, looking between us.

"Nothing," I said, at the same time Paul broke in.

"She saw a man at Ridgeline Trail after finding the body, and he turned up again at her hike today. Stood in the woods and stared at her."

Meggie grabbed my hand, squeezing it painfully.

"Tessa! You didn't tell me!"

I worked my hand out of her iron grip and winced, rubbing my joints.

"I didn't have a chance. This was way more important. It's fine. It's probably just a strange coincidence. You don't need to babysit me, Paul. I'm a big girl. I can look after myself."

Briar made a sound that sounded like a scoff and I glared at the cat in my lap.

"I know you can, Tess," Paul said, switching his tone. "But my heart can't take worrying about you. I'm coming with."

We stared at each other and I knew I'd already lost the battle before even beginning. Paul was pulling the older brother card and there wasn't a darn thing I could do about it. I sighed, shoulders slumping.

"Fine. But you don't have time."

"I'll make time."

"I can come too," Meggie said. "What time does the hike start?"

"Eight and you don't need to do that. You've got a business to run, Meggie. I'll be fine. Honestly."

"Well, the two of you need to be careful out there. I don't like this. Not one bit. What if he follows you through town and ends up at your house? Your vehicle is so distinctive with that warp. Everyone around here knows who you are."

I frowned and hugged Briar to my chest while Finn whined at my feet.

"Well, great. Now I've got something else to worry about. I'll be careful. Lock my doors. Finn won't let anyone near the house without warning me. It will be fine."

Paul and Meggie exchanged a glance, and I was right back to feeling like a child.

"I've been living on my own since I was eighteen guys. I can take care of myself," I added, frustration oozing out of every pore. "I've only seen him in the woods, and I don't think he has a car. That would be a very long walk to find my house. It's fine."

Meggie nodded, but I could see the worry in her eyes.

"Call me if you need anything, okay? You're out there in the middle of nowhere."

"You could stay at the new house," Paul said. "It's going to be a few weeks until I get everything sorted out."

As much as I loved the house Euphemia left Paul, there was no way I was staying there. I shook my head and stood.

"I appreciate it, Paul. Really. But I'll be fine."

"That's right. You have a new house," Meggie said, eyes wide as she looked at Paul. "What's it like?"

She was a goddess for distracting my brother. He settled back in his chair and began talking about all of its wonderful attributes while I squeezed past Meggie.

"I'll be next door and then I'm going home," I said, as Finn paused for Meggie to scratch her head. "See you two later."

I smiled to myself as I left the two of them together. The more time I could get them to spend together, alone, the more likely the two of them would realize they were perfect for each other.

I waved to Connie as I walked outside and walked a few steps to my office. I unlocked the door, flipped on the lights and hit the remote button for the mini-split system that served as my heater and air conditioner. A blast of cold air greeted my face, and I sighed in pure pleasure.

"I'm so glad I put that in," I said to the room at large.

I flopped into my seat and let Briar down to explore the small office while I turned on my computer. With the weekend coming, I'd be busy with two more hikes before I had another day off. Which would be spent helping Paul move. Tomorrow's hike would be at Ridgeline, and for the one on Saturday, I'd be over at one of my favorite places to hike, the loop around Prism Lake.

Finn leaned against my leg as I tapped on my keyboard, bringing up my email software to check on new bookings.

"They love you. That's why they worry so much," she said, her voice gentle.

I ran my fingers over the silky fur around her ears and nodded.

"I know. But I'm an adult. Sometimes Paul makes me feel like an incompetent child. I appreciate him, though. And love him. Even though he can be a pain."

"They're not ready, you know," Briar said as she leapt onto my desk and stared at the computer screen. "But keep pushing them together. Eventually, it will happen."

I stared at my cat, surprised that she'd picked up on my matchmaking efforts, and she gave me a kitty smile, her whiskers curving.

"You're pretty obvious."

I didn't know what to say to that, so I focused on my screen. My hike for tomorrow was already full, but there was a new booking for Saturday.

"Huh. Scott Trager booked with us again. Interesting. I didn't expect to see him again, especially this soon. He must have really enjoyed that hike."

"Mr. Muscles?" Finn asked.

"That's him. What did you think of him?"

She shrugged her shoulders and glanced at Briar.

"I never got close to him. There was something unfriendly about him, so I avoided him. How about you, Briar?"

"Same. You can always tell when someone's not an animal lover, and he's firmly in that camp. They send out spiky energy. Some cats like to mess with people like that, get them riled up, but I'm not one of them."

I looked at them, surprised at how little I truly knew about the inner workings of dogs and cats.

"You can feel that?"

Finn nodded before nipping at her flank.

"Every time. Those are the people who kick dogs when they think no one is looking. I stay far away."

I didn't want to know how she knew that. She'd been a mere pup when I'd adopted her at the shelter. A terrible thought made my blood run cold.

"No one's ever tried to kick you on one of my hikes, have they? I always try to watch both of you, but sometimes…"

"No, Tessa," Finn said, leaning hard on my leg. "Not with you. Never with you. You're the best human I've ever known."

My heart was in my throat as I stroked her head. Briar patted at my arm and I moved so she could crawl into my lap.

"Finn's right. I'm glad we waited for you."

She curled on my lap, purring, as I mastered my emotions. I'd always known there was something special about these two, and now? I couldn't imagine my life without them, or without being able to communicate with them. That made me think about Euphemia again. Her diary was at home, begging to be read, and I had plenty of time today to make that happen. I turned off my computer.

"Let's go home guys. I'll make lunch and then we can read Euphemia's diary. How does that sound?"

Finn let out a sharp yip of pleasure as I stood, cradling Briar. I turned everything off and headed back outside, eager to learn more about the woman who'd given me such a precious gift.

Chapter Sixteen

My alarm went off entirely too early, thanks to a late night reading through Euphemia's diary with Finn and Briar. We'd made it through the first few months of the last year of her life before falling asleep. Bittersweet was the only way to describe the way I'd felt after closing the diary for the night. Her words seemed to spring to life on the pages, offering a glimpse at a vibrant woman, who, while she'd been alone, had never been lonely. An intense longing stayed with me as I woke up, wishing I'd known her while she'd been alive.

While I might have been groggy, Finn and Briar certainly weren't, and were circling me by the time I stumbled to the kitchen and got the coffee going. We whipped through our morning routine and set out for the trailhead to meet my next group of hikers.

A shiver went down my spine as I reached the turnoff for the Ridgeline Trailhead. Had it only been a few days since I'd discovered the body? Somehow, It felt like a lifetime. I shook off the feeling and pulled into the lot.

Paul's Nissan truck was already sitting there, and I shook my head as I parked my rig. He was all smiles as he got out and stretched, rolling his neck before unleashing an explosive sneeze that made Briar's ears go back and Finn flinch.

"Sorry. Maybe I'll get all of my sneezes out before we start the hike. How many people do you have today?"

I gave him a look filled to the brim with doubt. Dragging Paul into the wilderness was a surefire way to ensure he'd be sneezing his head off until he got back to his car. He even found things to be allergic to in the dead of winter.

"Three. Small group today, but that will be nice. It should be a pretty smooth one. How did you sleep?"

He gave me a lopsided smile and tapped the side of his nose.

"The secret is not to go to sleep. I got the latest issue put to bed at four, and figured, what the heck, I'd keep slamming caffeine and just meet you here."

Well, that explained why he was so early. I frowned and folded my arms across my chest.

"Paul, you don't have to do this. You should be at home, tucked into bed. You can't run yourself ragged for me."

He pressed a kiss on the side of my head and ruffled my hair.

"Meh. I used to stay up all night and work all day right out of college. I'll be just fine. How long is today's hike?"

I opened the back of the Land Rover, freeing Finn and Briar, and started going through my pack, checking to make sure I had the essentials. I didn't have the heart to tell Paul that pulling an all-nighter and trying to function during the day was entirely different when you were in your thirties than your twenties, but I appreciated the effort he put in for me.

"We'll be out for our about three hours, so not very long. It will depend on the group, though. More experienced hikers means we can go farther."

I crossed my fingers and prayed we wouldn't have another couple like Tiffany and Jayden. A nice, complication free day would be amazing. Unlikely, but amazing.

"Did you have time to read through that diary I gave you?"

Paul leaned against the bumper and stroked Finn's head, getting her favorite spot right behind her left ear. Briar's fur brushed against my arm as I reached for the clipboard for the hike.

"I started it last night. Paul, I... I just can't believe we never knew her. She was here, right under our noses. From what I read last night, she watched over us, but never approached. She had to have been lonely. I'm just... Well, I'm mad at Dad. I can't believe he didn't let us make up our minds once we were older, you know?"

He nodded, but closed his mouth as a car pulled in. It was a newer, red sedan, and a woman was driving. She gave a cheery wave as she pulled into a parking space. I patted Paul's arm.

"We'll talk about it later. Show time."

The woman got out of her car and I glanced at the list on my clipboard. One more woman and a man were scheduled to arrive.

"Howdy," she said, her Texas drawl drawing out the words. "How y'all doing this fine morning?"

Her dark hair was set in perfect waves and her high-wattage smile could have supplied the grid with enough juice to fuel a neighborhood. Her brown eyes lit when she noticed Paul next to me.

"Good morning," I said, reaching out a hand that was ignored for a moment before she tore her eyes away from Paul and focused on me. "I'm Tessa Windsor, your guide, and this is Paul, my brother."

She purred out a breathy greeting in Paul's direction.

"Varsha Rockwell. It's nice to meet you. Looks like I'm the first one here. Oh, are these your pets?"

I nodded towards the back of the Land Rover.

"Yep. That's Finn, the border collie, and Briar is the cat. They always accompany me on these hikes."

"How darling."

She made no move to pet them as she adjusted the smart watch on her wrist. Her clothing was higher-end, and I took a quick glance at her feet. Name brand hiking books that had seen little action.

"Have you been on many hikes? I'll do a quick orientation once everyone else gets here, so you'll know what to expect."

"I live for the outdoors," she said, her eyes never leaving Paul's face. "How about you, honey? With a sister like this, I bet you love hiking."

Paul turned his head, sneezing loudly, and turned back with a sheepish grin.

"Not so much. I'm more of an indoors guy. Your accent says Texas. I'm guessing you're originally from Houston?"

"Not bad," she said, grinning, showcasing her pretty white teeth. "Galveston. Close enough, though. I moved up here after my divorce. It's been a little lonely, so I thought I'd get out here and meet some people."

I caught Briar's eye and nearly laughed at the expression pooling in those green depths. Paul might be oblivious to the hints Varsha was dropping, but my cat wasn't. Luckily, another car pulled in and I could excuse myself.

A woman stepped out of the SUV, her light brown hair tied back in a French braid that cascaded down her back. I put her in her mid-twenties and she had a spring in her step as she walked over.

"I hope I didn't make you wait too long," she said, her freckled face drawn in concern. "I was hoping to be early."

I smiled, liking her instantly.

"You are early. We're just waiting for one more. Tessa Windsor. I'm your guide for today's hike."

"Sara Turner. Nice to meet you. This is such a beautiful place. I can't wait to get on the trail."

"It's a beautiful hike. Not too strenuous, and plenty of magnificent views."

We walked back to join Paul and Varsha and I introduced them. Varsha's eyes slid over Sara before quickly dismissing her. She turned her attention back to Paul, and I bit my lip to hide my smile. Sara spotted Finn and turned to me.

"Yours? She's so beautiful. I love border collies. They're so much fun. Once I'm out of school and the dorm, I hope I can get one."

I readjusted her age to early twenties as I nodded.

"What's your major?"

"Psychology with a minor in criminal justice."

"Well, that sounds a lot more useful than the botany degree I got," I said, leaning against the side of my rig.

"I hope to join the police force when I graduate next year. It's hard to get hired, but it's been my goal. My dad was a detective in Denver."

I liked her even more. With any luck, she'd join the sheriff's department and give Jace a run for his money. A pickup pulled in and a young man hopped out, looked around and hurried in our direction.

"Sorry. I got lost and had to double back. Sam Friedman."

I gave him a sunny smile and shook my head.

"You're right on time. I'm Tessa Windsor, your guide. This is Sara, Varsha, and my brother Paul."

Sam shook everyone's hand and nodded before shoving his hands in the pockets of his khaki cargo pants.

"Nice to meet you. All of you."

I noticed he paid extra attention to Sara, his wholesome face lighting when she gave him a friendly smile. He wasn't exactly handsome, but he had a look about him that said he was someone you could trust. His brown curly hair was cropped short and his tanned face hinted he spent a lot of time outdoors.

"Alright everyone, let's go over everything you'll need to know about today's hike," I said, raising my voice a little to be heard over Varsha as she continued talking to Paul.

He shot me a pleading glance as I whipped through my orientation spiel. Once everyone was ready, we headed up the trail. I stuffed down the feeling of grief as I remembered the last time I'd climbed this route and the woman we'd found. The sun was shining, and today was a new day.

Varsha's voice came from behind as I led everyone out onto the trail, Finn at my side, and Briar walking next to us.

"It's just so nice to see a brother helping his sister."

"Oh my," Briar said. "She's laying it on a little thick, don't you think?"

"Well, Paul is single. Maybe she's nice," Finn said. "But her perfume makes me want to sneeze."

My brother must have gotten the same memo, as a thunderous sneeze sounded from behind us. Poor Paul. He really shouldn't have come with us, but part of me was glad he had. A prickling sensation kept my spine feeling as though a low level electrical charge was running through it as I passed a spot I remembered from my dream.

"So, are you from around here?"

That was Sam and I glanced back to see him walking next to Sara, checking his pace so she didn't have to walk too fast to keep up with him.

"Denver. I'm studying at the university here in town. How about you?"

"I work construction. Busy time of year, but I always like to get outside and be in nature. I'm from Grand Junction originally. Moved here after high school."

I focused back on the trail, hiding a smile. The two of them were hitting it off. Paul and Varsha? Maybe not so much. She was peppering him with so many questions about what he did. I took pity on him.

"Everyone, if you'll look over there, you'll see a rock formation made of gneiss rock. It's well over a million years old."

The appropriate oohs and ahhs echoed back, and I continued on, pointing out various interesting things. My feet slowed as I recognized where we'd ended up. Just to the left were the trees where I'd found the woman's body. I swallowed hard as the prickling sensation got worse. Maybe it would ease once I'd passed the spot.

"Up ahead, we've got some beautiful wildflowers that are still around. Typically, they peak in June, but up here, it's been cool enough that we still have quite a few. There'll be a meadow in the valley if you want to get some pictures."

"Oh, Paul, maybe you can take a picture of me once we get there," Varsha said, holding onto his arm with a talon-like grip. "And then maybe your sister could take one of us together. How romantic would that be?"

The glare Paul aimed at me slid off as I turned back to the trail and kept going. Instead of going away, the strange sensation was getting worse. I walked faster, forcing Finn to trot to keep up with me.

Once we were far enough ahead of the others, I slowed my steps.

"Do you guys feel that, or is it just me?"

"It feels like ants are crawling all over my fur," Finn said, stopping to scratch at a spot on her neck. "Briar?"

"Same. I don't like this. Not one bit. At first I thought it was just that woman's voice making my skin crawl, but I don't think so."

I frowned. I didn't know what it meant, but it was very uncomfortable. The voices of my group got louder as they closed the distance and I started moving again.

"It's just this weird feeling."

"You're telling me," Briar muttered.

We got through the narrow section of the trail, lined with trees, and the meadow opened up, revealing a beautiful expanse of native grasses sprinkled with a few wildflowers still clinging to their blooms.

"Here we are, everyone," I said, turning back to the trail. "We'll take a quick break here so you can get pictures if you'd like."

"Would you mind taking one of us?" Sam asked, nodding towards Sara. "I'd like to remember this spot."

From the flushed look on Sara's cheeks, she appreciated the gesture. I gave them a friendly smile and took Sam's phone, waving for them to move back. I crouched down in the grass, making sure I had a good angle, while Varsha posed a few feet away.

"Here you go," I said, handing his phone back to him.

Sara went up on her tiptoes to see the screen and Sam gave her a gentle smile.

"I could send a few of these to you, if you'd like. This one is my favorite. See the way the sun's hitting your hair?"

A soft woof from Finn drew me away from their conversation and I turned to see my pets a few feet away, staring at a spot in the treeline behind us. I walked over to join them, kneeling down to stroke Finn's head.

"What's up?"

"He's back."

I swallowed hard and squinted, finally spotting the man in the trees. He walked forward, hands up in the air.

"I think he just wants to talk," Briar said. "I'm not sensing danger from him. Or ill intent."

The man motioned for me to come near. He was close enough now that I could make out the pleading expression on his face. I glanced over my shoulder towards Paul, where he was occupied, taking more pictures of Varsha. Sam and Sara had their heads bent together, the strands of their hair tangling in the soft breeze.

"You're certain?" I asked Briar.

"As I can be. We're with you. You've got your pack. Let's see what he wants."

My feet seemed to pull me towards the treeline before I had a conscious thought of moving. Finn walked stiffly next to me, every line of her body tight as the man moved towards us. He slung the brightly colored pack down and raised his hands again, as if to say he meant no threat. I could only hope that was true.

Chapter Seventeen

Anxiety twisted my stomach into tiny knots as we approached the man. Now, I was close enough to see that his thin face was covered by several days' growth of beard. His eyes, light blue, still had that pleading look. His throat bobbed as I pulled Finn to a halt about ten feet from the man. Far enough away that we could run back to our group if he made one wrong move in our direction. I checked over my shoulder, where I could still see everyone, and looked back at the man.

"Why are you following us?"

"I'm sorry. I won't hurt you. I'm sorry if I scared you. It took me a long time to work up the courage to talk to you."

"Why? What do you mean?"

He shifted, and I noticed just how thin he was. He was taller than me, but weighed about the same amount, if my guess was right. His pants bagged on his stick-like legs. The jacket he was wearing hung open, revealing a worn t-shirt that billowed out from his sides.

"You were here. The other day. I... I saw you with the police. You found the woman, didn't you?"

I glanced over my shoulder and by the time I looked back, I

almost cried out with fright as I saw Briar approach the man. She sat at his feet, looking at him. A soft smile slid across the man's face and he knelt, holding out his hand to my cat.

"Hi, kitty. I won't hurt you. Or your mama. I just want to talk, okay?"

My breath froze in my chest as Briar sniffed his hand. She turned to me, her green eyes carrying a message to Finn. She pulled on the lead and I moved closer until she could sniff his shoes. He patiently waited for them to finish.

"I hope I passed inspection," he said, his lined face breaking into a smile. "They're real friendly animals. I used to have a dog. A real nice lab. Named him Jimmy. He was my buddy. He died of cancer last year."

A wave of sorrow broke in the man's eyes and any last shred of worry fled as I looked at the man. Really looked at him. He had to be almost seventy. He'd lived rough for a while, but it was obvious he was clean. The faint hint of peppermint soap reached my nose as he stood back up.

"I think you passed just fine. I'm Tessa Windsor. What's your name?"

"Arthur Callahan. But you can call me Art."

"Well, Art. You're right. I found the woman the other day. I spotted you then, at the trailhead. Why didn't you come talk to me?"

He wrung his hands together and stared at his well-worn boots. Briar surprised me again by getting closer and brushing his leg with her side. Finn sat at his feet, looking up at him with her soulful brown eyes. He seemed to relax.

"I was scared."

He spoke so softly I almost missed what he said. I inched a little closer.

"Why, Art? Why were you scared?"

"I saw it. I saw him kill her. It was terrible. I should've stopped him, but I was scared. He was a big dude. The woman... she was so small. She didn't stand a chance. I wanted to help her... But I..."

Tears sprang to my eyes as he talked, his eyes fastened firmly on mine.

"It's okay to be scared, Art," I said, swallowing the lump in my throat. "I get scared, too. What did you see?"

He turned his head, back down the way we'd come, and his thin shoulders shook.

"I was camped, back there in the trees. I sleep out here when the weather's good. It helps, you know. Seeing the stars at night. Makes me feel like I'm still free. I woke when I heard a scream. I thought it was a cat. Not this kind," he said, nodding at Briar with a shadow of a smile. "A big cat. But it wasn't. It was that woman. I crept through the trees and saw the man standing over her. He had his hands on her throat. She fought, but she couldn't get free. If I'd done something, anything, she still might be alive. He killed her and dragged her over to that place where you found her. I wanted to help, miss. Honest I did. But..."

"It's okay, Art. You're doing what you can now. This man, who killed her, he was scary. He wasn't right. He'd been stalking her for miles. Intent on ending her life. If you'd tried to intervene, he might have killed you, too."

If he thought it was strange that I knew so many details, he said nothing, but he nodded, and looked at Briar.

"I stayed hidden in the trees until I was certain he was gone. I wanted to check on her, but I knew from the way he dragged her, she was dead. I hid there, watching and waiting, until I saw you. And then the big deputy came. I wanted to tell the police, but I... Well, they don't take kindly to people like me. I don't hurt anyone. I just want to be free. But they get real mad when they find a guy out in the wilderness. I didn't want to go to jail. What if he thought I killed her? But I didn't, Tessa. I swear I didn't."

He was shaking so badly, I quickly closed the distance and put a gentle hand on his arm. He startled and looked at me, his eyes full of tears.

"I know you didn't, Art. You've got to tell the police, though. Maybe, with your help, they can find this man. They can stop him from doing it again. Felicity deserves that."

"Was that her name?"

"We think so, yes."

"That's a beautiful name."

"If it will help, Art, I'll go with you. To talk to the police. I can give you a ride. You won't have to do it alone."

He shook like a leaf, his head going back and forth.

"No, no, no. I can't."

"What's going on? Tessa? Are you okay?"

Art froze, his eyes huge, as Paul's voice sounded behind us. I kept my hand on Art's arm, fearful he'd dash away, as I turned to look at my brother.

"Paul, I'm fine. This is Art. He wants to help us. He saw what happened to Felicity."

I shot a pleading look at my brother, and while the wariness didn't leave his eyes, he relaxed his posture and crossed his arms over his chest.

"Hi, Art."

I turned to look at the man, his eyes as wide as a deer in headlights, poised to run. I softened my grip on his arm as he shook.

"Art, it's okay. Paul won't hurt you. He's my brother. He's just being protective."

Paul gave the man a tight smile and a quick bob of his head.

"Hi, it's okay. As long as you don't hurt my sister, you've got nothing to worry about from me."

I widened my eyes at Paul. Not what I had in mind for putting Art at ease. Finn woofed softly and pawed at Art's feet. He looked at her, and slowly, he stopped trembling. He gave my brother a shaky smile.

"I wouldn't dream of hurting her. I wouldn't hurt anyone," he said, before turning back to me. "But I can't go to the police. They'll lock me up. I just know it. I can't be behind walls, under roofs. I just can't. I need to be free."

I chewed on my lip. I didn't know this man's story. I didn't know what he might have done in the past that made him so worried about facing the police, but I knew he didn't kill the woman. Now that I was close enough, it was clear he wasn't the same man as the one I'd dreamt. No, this was a broken man who deserved kindness. He was trying to do the right thing. I just needed to figure out how to help him.

"You can ask Jace to meet us somewhere, instead of taking him in," Briar said, her voice soft.

I nodded.

"Art, what if I get the deputy you saw to agree to meet with you outside? I can sit with you while you talk. You don't have to go anywhere. We can get him to come to you."

Finn leaned against his leg, her tail wagging slowly as she looked up at him with those impossibly sweet brown eyes. Art ran a shaky hand over her head before looking back at me. His prominent Adam's apple bobbed as he nodded.

"That might be okay."

Relief coursed through me and it felt like the sun breaking through the clouds after a heavy rain.

"Great. Great. I can call him now and have him meet us at the trailhead."

Alarm flashed through Art's eyes and he backed up a step, nearly falling over Finn. He put his hands up.

"No. Not today. I'm not... I'm not ready. Tomorrow. I can do tomorrow. There are a few things I need to do first. Just... just in case."

I glanced at Paul, who shrugged and looked over his shoulder towards our hiking group. They were clumped together, staring at us with wide eyes. I couldn't take the chance that Art would flee, disappearing into the wilderness, never to talk with us again. My hike tomorrow was scheduled to begin at Prism Lake at ten. I could make this work.

"Okay, Art. That's fine. Tomorrow. I can meet you here at eight. I'll bring some food."

The mention of food brought a sharp gaze of longing into Art's eyes. He gave me a hesitant nod.

"I can do that. You don't have to bring food, though. I don't want you to go to any trouble on my account. I make do."

I didn't know how this poor man was feeding himself. From the looks of him, it was a struggle. My heart clenched, and I slung my pack off my back and rummaged through it, coming up with a handful of protein bars that I always carried. I handed them over, closing the distance between us.

"Here. I've got plenty of extras. Please. Take them."

Art's hand came up, and I carefully placed the bars across his palm. His eyes cleared as he looked at me, and for a moment, I saw the man he once was, before his past drove him out here, to live wild.

"Thank you. I'll be ready. Tomorrow. I won't let you down."

"I'll see you then, Art. Be careful out there, okay?"

He nodded, gave Finn one more pat on the head, picked up his backpack and faded back into the trees, clutching the protein bars. I let out a sigh, my shoulders slumping, and Paul put an arm around my shoulders.

"You handled that really well, Tess. I'm proud of you."

He pressed a kiss onto the side of my head and my heart swelled with love for this overprotective brother of mine.

"I guess we'd better get back, huh?"

"Yeah, probably should. This time, you get to walk with Varsha, though. I'll shepherd the two love birds."

Briar sprang ahead of us, pulling on her light lead, as Finn trotted to catch up to her. The three hikers were staring past us, into the woods where Art disappeared. Sam frowned as we approached.

"Was that man okay? Did he need anything?"

"I gave him some protein bars. He's alright. No one to worry about. Sorry for the interruption, guys. Let's continue our hike."

"People like that should be locked up," Varsha said, her pretty face twisted into a scowl. "They're a danger to the rest of us civilized folk."

I couldn't hide the flash of pure dislike as I looked at her. I didn't care. She was one customer I wasn't afraid to lose.

"That's a very narrow-minded way to look at things. He was perfectly harmless. Let's go everyone."

Sam and Sara gave her a wide berth as we continued down the trail. Varsha moved towards Paul, but he jogged ahead to catch up with me, leaving her at the back. I turned away and focused on the surrounding scenery, doing my best to continue the educational portion of the hike, all the while praying that Art wouldn't back out. We had a name for the woman, and now we had someone who'd seen her killer. We were getting closer to solving this case, but everything hinged on Art, a man who just wanted to be left alone.

Chapter Eighteen

I'll confess my hiking tour was the last thing on my mind, but I somehow pulled myself together and got everyone back to the trailhead. Paul had done his level best to avoid Varsha, but I had to hand it to the woman. If perseverance wasn't her middle name, it should have been. By the time we were all standing in front of our vehicles, she handed him a business card with a wink and a promising smile.

I cared more about Sam and Sara, and watched as they stood behind their cars, staring at the ground, neither one willing to be the first to go. Briar nudged my leg and nodded in their direction. Her hint was all too clear. I approached the couple and waited for them to notice me. It took a few seconds, but Sara finally turned, tilting her head to the side. I jumped in before she could speak.

"If you guys wanted to grab lunch, Robin's Roost is a great place to go. They've got an outdoor patio that would be lovely on a day like today. Just tell Meggie I sent you and she'll give you a discount on your lunch."

Sam's cheeks pinked a little, but he turned to Sara as he stuffed his hands in his pockets.

"What do you think? Want to have lunch? My treat?"

Her soft smile spoke volumes, and I wished them both well, and headed back to the Land Rover where Paul had retreated. He was busy arranging things, while Varsha gave him another meaningful look before getting in her car.

"Got one on the hook, huh?" I asked, elbowing him in the ribs.

"Oh gosh, don't start. Is she gone yet? I'm scared to look and potentially make eye contact."

I snorted and shook my head.

"She's pulling out now. You're safe."

His shoulders eased, and he stopped pretending to move stuff around in the back. I tossed my pack in before moving aside so Finn and Briar could jump in. Finn turned around twice and sank down, while the cat sat, curling her tail around her haunches.

"Well, do you think Jace is going to go for it?" she asked, turning to nip at her flank as Paul leaned against the bumper.

"You don't have fleas, do you? Do I need to give you a bath?"

She stopped what she was doing and fixed me with a glare.

"I do NOT have fleas. And I do not need a bath. I can't believe you would even suggest such a thing. I'll have you know..."

"Sometimes baths can be fun. Especially when it's hot out," Finn interrupted, giving her friend a doggy smile.

Briar's glare shifted over to Finn while my dog woofed out a soft laugh. Paul cracked a smile before turning to sneeze, sending Briar's ears back. He turned and wiped his nose with his forearm, ignoring my grimace.

"I don't have to hear them to know that your idea went over like a lead balloon. Sorry about the sneeze."

I rummaged in the back for a rag and handed it over.

"Here. Your arm's got some stuff on it. Okay, you two. Fine. No baths for Briar. But to get back to the point, I hope Jace will agree. If he doesn't, this plan is in the dumpster and I don't know what to do."

Paul wiped at his arm and handed the rag back. I wrinkled my nose and shoved it back towards him.

"Keep it. On the house."

"Do you want me to call him? He might take it better coming from me," Paul said, folding up the rag to stuff in his pocket.

I drummed my fingers on the bumper and shrugged.

"I don't know. I promised Art I'd be here. I should be the one to do it."

"I won't fight you for the honor, that's for certain. But hey, you're bringing him a potential lead that could crack the case. You think he'd be grateful."

"You've met Jace, right?" Briar asked, frowning so hard the white stripe down the center of her nose nearly disappeared.

I chuckled and translated for my brother before reaching for my phone.

"No point in putting it off, right? Like a bandaid. Just rip that sucker off and hope for the best."

I dialed Jace's number and waited, wishing the swirly feeling in my stomach would go away. I'd had to deal with him way more than I liked to for the past few days.

"Tess, what's up?"

"Jace, I've got someone you need to talk to about the murder case. He said he saw the killing take place, and he's willing to come forward."

Silence fell. Paul gave me a questioning look, and I shrugged, glancing at my screen to make sure the call didn't drop.

"Jace?"

"I'm here. So, how did you find this guy?"

"You know the guy I mentioned seeing twice? He finally approached me and told me his story. I think it's legitimate."

I knew it was, but there was no way I could say that. I could only hope he'd believe me and agree to the plan.

"I see. And he didn't feel the need to contact the police like a proper citizen would? He went to a woman who runs a hiking business?"

I bristled at his angry tone and fought to keep my temper in check.

"He knows I found the body. He must have been watching from the trees. I think he lives out here. Look, I know it's a little abnormal, but he's willing to come forward. Give him the benefit of the doubt."

"I don't have to do anything," Jace growled, his tone setting my teeth on edge. "You're gonna take the word of some cracked out homeless guy? Come on, Tess. You're smarter than that. Well, maybe you're not."

I ground my teeth together so hard my jaw popped.

"I'm plenty intelligent. Minus a lapse in judgement about thirteen years ago. He saw something, Jace. I believe him. At least hear him out. It was nearly impossible to get him to agree to this."

He heaved a sigh that blew through the phone line, irritating me further.

"Fine. Is he there now?"

Here was the sticky part. Paul leaned closer.

"No. He agreed to meet you here, at the Ridgeline Trailhead, at eight in the morning tomorrow. I'll be here to help. He's very... Well, I think he's been through a lot and he's a little jumpy. He seems to trust me, though."

"Oh great. So, I have to bend to the whims of a homeless dude and a woman who thinks she can solve all the world's problems, huh? I'm a busy man, Tessa. I can't just go haring off to follow dead-end leads."

Paul's eyes went flat, a sure sign he was about to blow his lid, and took the phone from my hand.

"Listen here, Deputy Roberts. I'm certain the townspeople of Collinsville would be interested in reading about how law enforcement refused to meet with a potential eyewitness to a murder. You'll be here at eight tomorrow or I'll run the story. Bottom line."

I blinked several times, shocked by Paul's vehemence. Finn and Briar were staring at him, too.

"Put Tess on the line."

Paul handed the phone back, and I cleared my throat.

"Yes?"

"I'll be there. So help me if this is a waste of time I'll arrest you for obstruction. Got it?"

He ended the call, and I swallowed hard as I tucked my phone away. I gave Paul a shaky smile.

"He'll be here. Hopefully I won't be leaving in his cruiser. If that happens, promise me you'll come get Finn and Briar. I can't handle it if they try to take them to the shelter. Maybe I should leave them at home."

Finn shot to her feet and a sharp bark echoed through the inside of the Land Rover.

"No! We go with you."

I put a steadying hand on her shoulder.

"But Finn..."

"I'll come with. He can't arrest us both, can he? Besides, I don't like the idea of you being alone with Art," Paul said, holding up a hand at my gasp of outrage. "I know he seems nice and harmless, but still. I'll be here."

I frowned, but nodded.

"Fine."

He gave me a reassuring smile and tucked me into a one-armed hug.

"That's the spirit. What's your plan for the rest of the day?"

"Home. Lunch. Probably read more of the diary. How about you?"

"I've gotta wrap up a few things in the office and then head home to continue packing up my stuff. Sunday's the big day."

I pushed aside all my worries once I saw the look on Paul's face. He was truly excited about his new house and he didn't need me being a big, wet blanket.

"And I'll be there to help you move. I can't wait to see what you're going to do to the place. It's an epic house."

"It is, isn't it? Look, I've got an idea or two I want to follow up on about this case. I'll let you know if I find anything, okay? Later, Tess."

And with that enigmatic statement, he waved and hopped into his pickup, not giving me a chance to ask questions. I watched him leave and turned to my pets.

"Shoot. I wonder what he's working on?"

"Who knows? We'll figure it out, though," Briar said, stretching. "I'm ready for lunch and a nice nap."

I got everything packed away, got them settled, and jumped in the driver's seat to get us home. One of the best things about running your own business was the ability to take time off, and I couldn't wait to dive back into Euphemia's diary.

Once we were home, I let Finn out to ramble, amazed by the amount of energy she had after our hike, and got Briar inside. She hopped onto the coffee table where she could see Finn zooming around outside.

I busied myself in the kitchen, getting their lunch made before working on mine. Given the state of my pantry and fridge, I went with a peanut butter and jelly sandwich, with some stale chips on the side. A soft scratch came from the front door and I let Finn in.

She was panting hard, but looked joyful as she careened into the kitchen to her water bowl. Loud slurping sounded and Briar gave a delicate shudder.

"She gets water everywhere."

She hopped down and joined her friend in the kitchen, where I served up their lunches, side by side, with their special bowls. I tucked into my sandwich while I stood there and munched through my chips. Once the last scrap of food had been licked up, and Finn devoured my crusts, I got the dishes washed.

Finn and Briar were already on the couch, waiting for me, as I dried my hands and joined them.

"Alright. Where were we?"

"I think you were just finishing the entries for March," Briar said, settling onto her favorite couch cushion.

Finn stretched out on the floor on her side, eyes heavy, while I cracked open the diary and settled into the corner of the couch to read, tucking my feet underneath me. I paged through until I found the end of March and began reading.

I was halfway through April when I sat up straight with a gasp when I spotted my name. Finn raised her head, eyes wary, and looked around.

"What? I heard nothing."

Briar cracked an eye and gave me an expectant look.

"Listen to this, guys. The longer I watch Tessa, the more certain I am of my decision to pass on my gift to her. Her affinity with her animals, and her love of nature seem to hint to me she contains some earth magic, but it will be interesting to see how she manifests. I wish I could be here to see it. I can only hope her father hasn't poisoned her mind against me. If she says no, or the gift doesn't find her worthy, it will dissipate, like dust in the wind. Centuries of our family's history, gone in an instant. I have faith, though. She'll rise to the challenge. I've found no one else more worthy to carry this gift. I wish I could talk to her, guide her somehow. But I have to trust that she will find her own way. Like I did. I only regret that I won't be around to see it when it happens."

I put the book down as emotion clogged in my throat. She'd been watching me? She found me worthy?

"Wow," Finn said, her voice breathy. "Centuries of history. I'm glad you said yes, Tessa. That would've been a shame."

I nodded as tears ran down my face. If Paul hadn't opened the box, if the lightning bug, or whatever it was, hadn't found me worthy, I wouldn't be sitting here, having a conversation with my beautiful animals. I wouldn't have had that dream about Felicity's death. Nothing would be the same.

Briar's soft paw touched my arm, and I opened them so she could climb into my lap, snuggling close. Her purrs vibrated through my chest, easing a bit of the pain away.

"She knows you did it. I can feel it. Who knows? Maybe one day she'll appear and you can talk to her."

"I wish I could say thank you," I said, stroking her fur. "I never even knew her, but I wish I could thank her properly."

"You can," Finn said, resting her head on my foot. "Just because she's gone doesn't mean she doesn't know. And maybe Briar's right. Maybe you'll see her. Somehow. Anything is possible."

Her words echoed through my heart as I picked up the diary and began reading again. Euphemia's words seemed to jump from the page, burrowing deep within my heart. Maybe they were right. Maybe she knew. I could only hope she did.

Chapter Nineteen

I woke up well before the sun rose the next morning, too excited about meeting with Art to sleep well. As I shifted beneath the covers, Briar let out an irritated sigh while I could feel Finn's tail thumping on the bed. Finn was always cheerful when she woke up, no matter what time it was. Briar? Not so much.

"Will you stop wiggling and just get up?" she hissed, resettling her paws underneath her. "And then I can grab a few more minutes of sleep before we go. I don't know if you're aware, but cats need around sixteen hours of sleep per day, and I've been dangerously short lately."

I stroked her long fur and rubbed under her chin, the one spot guaranteed to put her in a good mood.

"Sorry, baby. I'm just antsy. I hope this meeting goes well. You know how Jace is. He's ornery on a good day. I don't want him scaring Art."

"It will be okay, Tessa," Finn said before launching off the bed, her nails skittering on the wood floor. "Let's go! A run will sort everything out."

She was running down the hall before I swung my legs out of

bed. Briar grumbled and licked at her paw, muttering about early birds and worms.

I followed Finn, let her outside, and doubled back to the kitchen to make some coffee. Finn's delighted shouts echoed back through the valley as she sprinted off. I couldn't help but smile at her sounds of pure joy. Once the coffee was dripping, I headed outside, grabbing a hoodie off the coat rack as I passed it.

I pulled it on and shoved my feet in my sandals, heading off the porch to see where Finn was. A streak of black and white fur in the nearby trees caught my attention.

"So much energy," Briar said, appearing next to me on the porch, before yawning.

"I thought you were gonna catch a little more sleep."

She gave a kitty shrug, stretched and trotted down the steps.

"Like I can sleep with that ruckus going on."

"Wheeeee," came Finn's shout as she careened past. "Morning, Briar."

I thought about going for our usual walk, but I needed to hit up the grocery store before I left for the trailhead. The one on the outskirts of town was open twenty-four hours a day, and I wanted to grab a few things for Art. I wasn't sure he'd accept them, but I had to try.

"Alright guys, let's go back in. I'll fix your breakfast."

I'd barely finished my sentence and Finn was already on the porch, shaking off her fur while grinning.

"That was fun."

Briar trotted in behind Finn, and they were waiting for me in the kitchen as I closed the door. Once their breakfast was eaten and I'd cleaned up, we were ready to hit the road. I grabbed my pack and headed out, locking the cabin door behind me. If everything went well, I'd be back here later, after the hike, with plenty of time to read more of the diary.

Finn circled Briar as they waited for me to open the door to the Land Rover. The cat was still a little grouchy, but she perked up as I told her my plans to get Art some extra food that he could take with him.

"That's very nice of you, Tessa. Some protein granola mix would be great for him. Lightweight, but packed full of nutrition."

I smiled into the rearview mirror as I backed out and we headed for the store. It didn't take me long to whip through my list, and I grabbed a box of donuts on my way to the check-out station. One never passes up donuts when one doesn't have to.

I stowed everything but the donuts in the back and Finn was sniffing, her brown eyes wide, as I got in the driver's seat.

"Oh, those smell delicious."

Even Briar leaned forward to get a deep sniff as I headed for the trailhead, donuts stowed on the dash.

"Do I smell bear claws?"

"Yep. The cherry kind."

"Yum," Finn said, swiping her muzzle with her tongue. "I love those."

The roads were empty as I drove to the trailhead, feeling as though I was trapped in an unending cycle of ending up in this place. Paul's truck was already there, and I could see him tapping away on his laptop as I parked next to him. He gave me an absent-minded wave until I knocked on the window, holding up the box of donuts.

"Ooo, donuts," he said, rolling down the window with a grin. "My favorite sister."

"I'm your only sister, but thanks, I guess. Whatcha working on? A story for the paper?"

Paul's grin slid off his face as his eyebrows knit together in a frown. He took a donut and in one massive bite, half of it was gone.

"I was thinking last night about this case and did a little searching. If we're right, and that was Felicity who was murdered, she's not the only one. I found a string of missing redheads in the tri-state area who've ended up dead. This is bad, Tess. Terrible."

My stomach shriveled into a tiny ball, all thoughts of donuts long gone.

"No. A serial killer?"

"I'm afraid it might be. What time is it?"

I checked my watch and turned it towards him.

"Almost eight. Art should be here soon. And Jace. Are you going to tell him what you found?"

"I have to. I'd hope he already discovered it in the course of his investigation, but I have to tell him."

I nodded and stepped back from his truck, moving towards the back of the Land Rover in a daze. I juggled the box as I got the door open, revealing a worried Finn and Briar. I heard Paul's door open, and he joined us, taking the box from my numb hands. He dug another donut out, ignoring the hopeful look Finn shot his way while he crammed it in his mouth. Paul and I were a lot alike, but how we handled stress was entirely different. He preferred to eat his feelings, while I preferred to stuff them deep down inside, where they stewed in my stomach, making eating impossible. What can I say? We're not the best at coping at things.

I handed him a napkin and pointed to his mouth.

"You've got a bit of glaze right there," I said, before looking around the trailhead, hoping to spot Art. "He's coming, right?"

Paul shrugged and polished off the last of his bear claw. Finn heaved a sigh and sank down. I reached into the box, pinched off a corner of one, and tossed it to her. She grabbed with a snap before bolting it down.

"Thanks, Tessa," she said, after swiping away the crumbs from her muzzle.

At least my dog was a tidy eater. The same could not be said for my brother. Briar shifted, wrapping her tail around her feet tightly.

"I hope he shows. He was so nervous yesterday," she said, her eyes following the same track mine did. "I don't smell him, though. He's not close by."

The sinking feeling in my stomach got worse, and I waved off the donut box Paul shoved in my direction.

"No, thanks. Better save at least a few for Art. He's gotta show up. He promised me."

I avoided looking at Paul, preferring not to see the expression in his eyes. He put down the box and leaned against the bumper, brushing the crumbs off his tee.

"We'll hope for the best. Did you read the diary yesterday?"

I clung to the change of conversation like a life raft and nodded.

"I did. She mentioned me, Paul. She hoped we'd accept her gifts, and that the magic would pass to me. I feel like she knew us, but we never got that opportunity. It feels weird. To be honest, I'm mad at Mom and Dad."

"Mad or just very disappointed?"

I elbowed him in the side and rolled my eyes. That line always worked on us when we were kids and got into trouble, but the more I thought about it, I realized he was right. I was disappointed with our parents.

"I just wish they'd let us decide on our own, you know? Oh well, there's nothing we can do about it now."

"Look alive, here comes Jace."

I looked around the parking lot again, praying I'd see Art's lanky form approaching, but the place was silent. Jace drove his cruiser into the parking spots across from us, and that old sinking feeling came roaring back. What would he do if Art didn't show?

Jace heaved himself out of his vehicle and adjusted his duty belt underneath his protruding belly before slamming the door and strolling our way. Paul sighed, but I tried to paste a smile on my face. I knew it was fake, and I didn't care. Chances were, Jace wouldn't notice, anyway. He'd never been able to read my emotions.

"Well, well, well, look who's here," he said, his voice overly loud. "And more importantly, look who's not."

He crossed his beefy arms across his chest and stared at me, his expression unfriendly until he spotted the box of donuts sitting in front of Finn. I fought the urge to step in front of them and block his access, but I knew we needed him on our side.

"I'm sure he's coming," I said, making my voice as bright as possible. "Donut?"

"Don't mind if I do," he said, waggling his thick fingers. "What do we have here? Bear claws, huh? No Boston Creams?"

"No. Chocolate's bad for dogs and cats and I like to share with them," I said.

His lip curled, but he shrugged and grabbed a donut, giving it a careful eye, likely thinking it would be covered in pet hair. He took a bite and Paul cleared his throat.

"Jace, I've discovered something troubling, and I think it might have something to do with this case."

"You mean the fact that your sister wasted my time and dragged me out here early with her supposed eye witness who probably doesn't even exist?"

My eyes went narrow and my whole body tensed.

"Art is real. He said he would be here. We need to give him more time. The poor guy might just be running late."

"If you say so, Tessa. What are you talking about, Paul? Got another crazy lead for me to follow?"

Paul's jaw tensed, but he kept his voice neutral.

"A crazy lead like discovering the name of the woman who was killed before you did? No, this is something else. I did a little digging and found a disturbing pattern. Several women, matching the overall description of the woman killed here, have been found dead, and more are missing. We're talking Nebraska, New Mexico and Kansas, Jace. I think there's a pattern going on."

Jace munched through the rest of his donut, wiped his hands on his uniform pants, and looked at Paul. I knew Jace well enough to tell he was about to lie to us.

"Interesting. I, of course, can't comment on an ongoing investigation. I'm certain you know that, Paul, given that you're pretending to be a journalist."

I stepped forward, trying to diffuse the storm I could feel coming from Paul after Jace's nasty words landed hard.

"Jace, there's no need to be rude. Are we dealing with a serial killer or not?"

Jace swung back towards me, his blue eyes narrowed.

"I can neither confirm nor deny that information," he said, spitting out his words like they were tinged with acid. "And you both need to be very certain that this information does not leak out."

"What about freedom of the press?" Paul asked, his color high as he faced off against Jace. "What about the public's right to know if they're in danger? This is serious, Jace. If we've got a serial killer in our midst, who's saying they won't strike again?"

"We're working on it, okay? If I see even a hint of that in your paper, I'm coming for you, Windsor. You cannot disturb an active investigation. We've got protocol, and you could tromp all over it."

I exchanged a glance with my brother. Obviously, he'd hit a nerve and that meant Paul was absolutely right. I diffused the argument the only way I knew how. I grabbed the box of donuts and held it out to Jace.

"Another one?"

He knew dang well what I was doing, but that didn't stop him from grabbing another bear claw. The only thing Jace liked more than being an irritating jerk was eating. I stole a quick look at my watch and my shoulders slumped. It was already half-past eight and no sign of Art. I looked hopefully towards the trees where I'd seen him the first time, but came up empty.

Paul followed my line of sight and shook his head slightly. Art wasn't coming. My next hike was far enough away that I needed to leave in a few minutes or I'd be late. I'd be cutting it pretty close as it was.

"Well, this was a colossal waste of my time," Jace said, as he helped himself to a third donut. "But at least I got some free food. You want the rest of these?"

I rolled my eyes and handed over the box. My appetite was shot and after he'd had his mitts on them, I didn't want them.

"No. Take them. I'm sorry, Jace. I was so certain he'd show up. Art saw something. I know he did. If we can get him to talk, he could work with a sketch artist or something. Maybe even pick someone out of a lineup."

"Yeah, and the Broncos might make it to the playoffs. I gave you the benefit of the doubt, Tess, and you let me down. If this guy is real, you're going to bring him to me. I won't do this again."

He took the box of donuts back to his cruiser and roared off, peeling out of the trailhead, tossing gravel everywhere with his tires. This time, I didn't bother to hide my sigh. Paul rubbed my arm and shook his head.

"You tried Tess. I'm sorry."

"What if something happened to him?" Briar said, looking at me with sad green eyes. "Art seemed honest. I don't think he meant to blow you off."

I looked around at the surrounding hills and swallowed the bad taste in my mouth. Sleeping the rough wasn't easy. What if the killer had somehow found out that Art saw him? He might have been silenced.

"I'll come back and look for him," I said, nodding at Briar. "But I've got to get to our hike. I'm sorry to drag you out here, Paul."

He gave me a sunny smile and ran a hand through his hair, spiking it up in all different directions.

"No worries, Tess. I've got to get to the paper, but I can help you look for him later on, okay? Don't come out here alone. It's not safe."

I nodded and closed the back door of the Land Rover, that bad feeling still hanging around like a noxious odor.

"Thanks, Paul. I'll call you when I'm done with my hike."

I hopped back in the driver's seat and headed out of the parking lot. Prism Lake was a beautiful hike, and I should have been looking forward to it, but all I could think about was the potential of a serial killer targeting people in my town, and Art. I glanced back at the trailhead in my rearview mirror and said a brief prayer that he was okay.

Chapter Twenty

We made it to Prism Lake with ten minutes to spare, and I quickly set to work, prepping for the hike. A quick check of my clipboard revealed I had three people scheduled for the loop around the lake. Scott Trager, otherwise known as Mr. Muscles, and two other men. A prickle went down my spine as I thought about what Paul said. A week ago, I wouldn't have thought twice about leading a hike with only men in the group, but now? Now I couldn't shake the feeling that something awful was about to happen.

Finn's cold nose nudged my hand, breaking me out of my thoughts.

"You okay, Tessa?"

I stroked her head and nodded.

"Sorry. I just have a bad feeling that I can't shake. It's probably because Art didn't show. I still can't believe he stood us up."

Briar sidled closer, leaning against my side.

"We have the same feeling. Be careful today, Tessa. Something is in the air and it's not good."

Well, that didn't help settle my nerves. Not one bit. I checked my pack, ensuring that I still had my gun. I spotted it inside its holster and shut the bag back up. I'd never had to use it on anything but targets at the shooting range, and honestly, I didn't know if I ever could. Faced with a life and death situation? Maybe. But the thought of taking someone's life sat in my stomach like curdled milk. I shook off that thought and turned as a vehicle rolled in.

The man behind the wheel waved, and I nodded in his direction, recognizing Scott Trager. He parked and ambled over, dressed much like he'd been the last time I'd seen him. This time, however, he wasn't carrying a hydration pack.

"Morning, Miss Windsor. Beautiful day, isn't it?"

I gave him a non-committal smile, half listening as a truck pulled in and backed into a spot. A man in his sixties got out and headed our way. The first thing I noticed about him was his bushy mustache and completely bald head. It was as though his hair follicles had all migrated right under his nose.

"Howdy. Burt Quinlan. I'm at the right spot, correct?"

"That's right, Burt. Nice to meet you. I'm Tessa Windsor, your guide for the day. And this is Scott Trager."

He nodded at Scott before focusing behind me.

"Would you look at that? Now that's a beautiful dog right there. I've got a German Shepherd at home."

Finn hopped out of the Land Rover, giving Scott a wide berth, and sat in front of Burt, wagging her tail on the ground. He knelt and gave her his hand to sniff.

"Real nice pup. How many other folks are joining us today, Miss Tessa?"

I liked this man immediately. From his accent, I guessed he was originally from somewhere in the southwest.

"One more, Burt. I'm glad you've taken a liking to Finn. She'll be coming with us. Briar will as well."

I didn't miss the way Scott backed up as Briar jumped out of the Land Rover and joined us, sitting next to Finn. She looked up at Burt with a bold expression in her eyes and he made a delighted crowing sound.

"Would you look at that? Are you sure you're a cat, little missy? You act like a dog. I don't mean no offense. Now, don't put your back up."

I smothered a smile as he let Briar sniff his hand. Even with the canine comment, it was clear she took an immediate liking to him as well. We all looked to the right as another vehicle pulled in. Burt stood and pivoted, and I noticed a holster at the back of his belt.

I took a step back, surprised, but he shook his head slightly as he noticed me looking.

"Never can be too prepared. Or safe, Miss Tessa."

I wasn't certain what it was, but there was something about Burt that made me trust him immediately. I focused on the last hiker as he approached. His pudgy face was a little flushed, but he gave all of us a friendly smile as he stuck out his hand towards Burt.

"Mike Porchek. Nice to meet you."

I pushed aside my concerns about Burt and shook Mike's hand. It was faintly moist, but I tried not to show my distaste as he beamed at me.

"This is my first hike. I promised my wife I'd get out and be more active, and well, here I am. I hope I won't hold you back. Where are we headed today?"

Scott groaned and turned away, causing Mike to frown faintly.

"I hope I didn't say the wrong thing. I saw the hike on the website. I was just trying to make conversation."

"It's fine, Mike," I said. "We'll be doing the loop around Prism Lake today. There's a bit of elevation gain at the start, but it levels out after that. It's a beautiful place to hike. I think you'll enjoy it."

I shouldered my pack and shut the doors of the Land Rover, glancing over at Scott as he paced near the start of the trail.

"No squats today?"

He looked at me, his face expressionless, and shrugged.

"Warmed up earlier."

Ah, now it made sense. There were no other women besides me to impress. I stifled a chuckle and turned towards Burt and Mike, waving them ahead, before clipping Finn and Briar's leads on.

"All right, everyone. Let's hit the trail."

I hadn't been kidding about the steep section at the beginning of the hike. My calves burned as I led everyone up the sharp rise, looking back every so often to check on everyone.

Conversation was limited to grunts and wheezes. Burt might have been a bigger man, with a hefty middle, but he kept right up with me, even on the most difficult portion of the trail.

"My mama always said I was part mountain goat," he said, tossing me a grin. "Maybe she was right."

Unfortunately, poor Mike Porchek was not as sure-footed. I glanced back again, noticing he was quite a ways down the trail, and whistled for Finn. She stopped, ears up, and immediately trotted back my way.

"She's a well-trained dog, isn't she?" Burt asked, wiping sweat off his bald head with a handkerchief, before stowing it in his back pocket.

"She's a marvel."

I couldn't help but remember Briar's comment about training the other day. I'd thought I'd been the one who'd taught Finn commands, but now? I think it might have been the other way around.

"C'mon, Finn. Let's go check on Mike."

Scott jogged past, giving the pudgy man a contemptuous smirk, and ignored me as I passed him on the way down. I slowed my steps and pulled up next to Mike.

"Just a little further and it levels out. You doing okay?"

He shot me a look brimming with embarrassment and nodded once, huffing and puffing. His face, beet red with exertion, was slick with sweat.

"I'm alive. I can do it. I just hope I can get back down."

I gave him an encouraging grin and shrugged.

"Down is the simple part. You've got this, Mike. Just a little further."

I stayed with him until we crested the rise. Prism Lake came into view and I took a minute to appreciate the sight, hands on hips, while Mike caught his breath. He was bent in half, but his face was now flushed with victory instead of exertion. Scott seemed unaffected by the climb, choosing to jog in place, fingers over the pulse in his neck.

"Thanks," he said, once his breathing slowed. "I appreciate you not making me feel like an out-of-shape loser."

He frowned in Scott's direction.

"Never, Mike. We're all at different points in our journey. The important thing is getting out there and taking that first step. Besides, the view's worth it, isn't it?"

He nodded and stood straight. Burt joined us, making a clucking sound.

"Now that's a purty view, ain't it? A guy could get used to seeing beauty like this. You did real good back there, Mike."

He gave the pudgy man a hearty clap on the back that sent Mike tumbling forward a few steps.

"Thanks, man."

"Alright everyone," I said, striding out with Finn, Briar trotting behind us with her tail high. "Let's do the loop around the lake. During this time of year, we should be able to spot some water ouzels, also known as American Dippers. They'll be found near the shallows of the lake. If you look up, you might also spot some golden eagles and prairie falcons."

Scott snorted and looked back.

"If it's alright with you, I'm gonna jog ahead. I need to keep my heart rate going."

I shrugged. While I typically liked to keep everyone together on a hike, I wasn't in any rush to keep him tied to the group. I didn't miss the unfriendly looks Finn shot him, and Briar's ears were flat. Never a good sign.

"Suit yourself. We can meet back at this spot."

He ignored me and headed out, spraying gravel from under his shoes as he sprinted down the trail.

"Youth is wasted on the young," Burt said, shaking his head. "Now, why would you wanna rush off when you can take in the glory of nature?"

"Different horses for different courses is what my mom would say," I said, smiling over at Mike. "You ready to go?"

"Let's do this," Mike said, giving me a determined nod. "I can breathe normally now. Well, almost."

It was easy to keep the two men entertained with facts about the local plants and wildlife, and the time passed quickly. A Stellar's Jay gave a raucous cry, delighting Burt as it flew past with a flash of its blue wings as we reached our original starting point.

"Would you look at that? Prettiest blue I've ever seen."

I couldn't help but share his joy as I watched the bird wing across the lake. Mike stood in a shaded portion of the trail, still flushed, but obviously happy at his achievement. I glanced around, frowning. Scott wasn't waiting for us.

"Looks like he decided not to wait, Miss Tessa," Burt said as he smoothed his mustache. "I can't say that's much of a loss, though. We'll probably catch up with him on the way down."

I frowned, but my scalp prickled uneasily as I looked around the lake. I'd lost sight of Scott about fifteen minutes ago. Had he gone back down without us? The last thing I wanted to do was leave someone behind, particularly if they were injured.

"I spotted him running this way when we were back there," Mike said, pointing off into the distance. "I think he left us."

"Alright, well, let's head back to the trailhead. Maybe he's waiting for us there."

The feeling of unease refused to leave, and I spent the rest of the hike looking around. Briar clung to Finn's harness, her green eyes keen as she looked through the trees. I desperately wanted to ask if they scented Scott, but Burt and Mike were too close for me to risk talking to them.

"Now what I don't understand is why a man would pay good money to go on a hike and then go off on his own," Burt said, mopping his head with his handkerchief again. "That just makes no sense."

"I hope I didn't irritate him," Mike said, as he gingerly picked his way down the steep trail. "He didn't seem friendly. I know I've slowed everyone down."

"Nonsense, Mike. You're doing great," I said, hoping to encourage the man. "I hope you've enjoyed it so far."

He nodded, giving me a tight grin as he nearly slipped on the path.

"It's been way more fun than I thought it would be. I think this is something I could get used to doing. I appreciate it, Tessa. You've been a great guide."

I couldn't help but beam at his praise as we made our way to the end of the trail. Scott Trager was nowhere in sight, but his car was still parked, three spaces down from mine. Burt looked around, hands on hips.

"Well, don't that beat all? I wonder where he is?"

"Maybe he's using the restrooms," Mike said, pointing towards the wooden structure. "I'd better go. Thanks again, Tessa. I'll have to book another hike with you. Maybe next time I'll get my wife to come along. She'd love it."

He waved and headed back to his car, limping a little. Burt frowned, chewing on the ends of his mustache.

"Want me to hang around with you until Scott comes back?"

I thought about it. Even though the sun was beating down and I was warmed up from the hike, a chill worked its way down my spine. But I shook my head. I needed to talk to Finn and Briar, and I couldn't do that with him around.

"No, that's okay, Burt. It was nice to meet you and I hope you had fun today."

"More fun than a barrel of monkeys has any right to have," he said, nodding. "All right, Miss Tessa. I'll get out of here. You take care of yourself, you hear?"

"Will do, Burt."

He waved and hauled himself into his pickup, firing up the throaty engine. He pulled out of the lot and I waited until I couldn't see the vehicle any more before turning to Finn.

"Do you smell him? Did we pass him on the trail? I don't think we can leave until we know for sure where he is. What if he got injured back there?"

"Well, once he headed off on his own, he ceased to be our responsibility," Briar grumbled. "I don't like that guy."

I glanced towards the restrooms and debated going over to knock on the doors. I didn't particularly like the man either, but I couldn't just leave. I heaved a sigh and tugged on Finn's lead.

"Let's go check. He's probably in there. Once we know he's safe, we can head home."

Finn's nails clicked on the asphalt as we walked towards the wooden structure. All I could hear were the sounds of the birds, and the soft wind rustling through the pines. I rapped on the door of the men's room.

"Scott? Are you there?"

Nothing. I debated opening the door and peeking in, but Finn barked sharply, startling me.

"He's there. He just left the trees."

I whipped my head around and spotted Scott moving fast. He was at my rig by the time we turned around and headed in his direction.

"There you are. I was worried about you," I said, not bothering to hide my irritation. "There are mountain lions in these woods. It's never a smart idea to separate from the group."

He bared his teeth in a grin and walked closer.

"There are more dangerous things in the woods than that."

Finn growled low in her chest as he approached, still wearing that grin. My heart began beating faster as I saw the look in his eyes. We were in trouble. Deep trouble.

"Tell that dog to shut up before I do it for you. Trust me, you won't like my methods."

Fear gripped my insides as he rushed towards us, hands outstretched towards my precious dog. Briar hissed, launching herself at the man, as Finn stood her ground, barking madly.

"Stop! What are you doing?"

I stepped between them, trying to force the much taller man back. Everything dissolved into a whirlwind of black and white fur, lashing claws, and a high-pitched bark that made my blood run cold. My world went black as the pavement rushed up to meet me.

Chapter Twenty-One

Time seemed to stop for a moment, to cease to have meaning, as I laid on the hard surface of the parking lot. Sounds filtered through the thick fog of my mind. A man, shouting. A cat, hissing and howling. A dog hoarsely barking. And through it all, the sound of a woman's voice. A voice I'd never heard before.

"Tessa. You must get up."

A bright light flared as the words repeated, becoming a chant that finally broke through my consciousness. For a split second, I was certain that the woman, whoever she was, breathed a sigh of relief as I opened my eyes.

My cheek, the one not pressed against the asphalt, burned, and my vision was hazy around the edges, but I was awake. I was alive. And so were Finn and Briar. From where I was, I could see Briar, crouched just a few inches away, tucked behind the wheel of my Land Rover. The cold nose shoved under my shoulder belonged to Finn, and she was desperately trying to get me on my feet.

"Come on, you've got to get up. He's coming back!"

Briar's hissed command tore through the rest of the haze and I came to, whipping my head to the right in time to see Scott Trager advancing towards us. I struggled to get to my knees, groping for the zipper on my pack, only to realize it was gone. There was nothing on my back.

"Looking for your gun?" Scott said, his face twisted in a sickly smile. "I took care of that. I thought about shooting the dog and cat with it, but I wanted to wait. It's more fun if you watch."

I put a hand on Finn's back as she tensed, ready to fly at the man facing us. I couldn't handle it if something happened to her.

"No. I don't care what you do to me, but you will not hurt them," I said, struggling to my feet.

He stepped closer, and I noticed he was wearing a flannel shirt over his tank top. A wave of nausea crashed over me as the smell hit me. I knew this smell. It was the horrible musk I'd smelled in my vision of Felicity's death. A bright red scratch marred his handsome face, blood smeared underneath it. It looked like Briar's claws hit their mark.

"Really? You think you can call the shots? I don't think you realize who's in charge here. And that's not you, little one. It's me."

I nearly swallowed my tongue at the phrase he used. Little one. That's what he'd called Felicity when he was hunting her down.

"I'm not little and you're not hurting them. Let them go. They've done nothing to you. They're innocent. It's me you want. I'm the one who knows you killed that woman."

His eyes sharpened as he focused on me.

"You weren't the only one, though. Luckily, I tied up that loose end last night. That bum won't be flapping his gums ever again. And soon, you won't either. That's right. I've been watching you. For days now. I saw you two talking in the woods. I saw him that night, the night I freed Felicity. I would've let him go, but he had to tell someone what he saw. He had to mouth off. So, I freed him too. Now it's your turn. The hair isn't right, but I'll make an exception. Just for you."

My stomach dropped as I realized he'd killed Art. He hadn't flaked on us at all. The poor man had been killed. What did Scott mean by freed? The way he said the word made my spine shake, but I fought down the fear before it could consume me.

"And they're not the only ones, are they?"

"Oh, looks like someone's been doing their research. Let me guess, your brother? Oh, I know all about you, Tessa Windsor. I did my research, too. You're thirty-one, single, overly attached to your pets, and your brother runs the paper in town. If I had more time, I'd free him too. But I'm guessing he'll be so broken-hearted by his beloved sister's death he won't be able to think straight. It will give me the time I need to get out of town. It's a shame. I'd never killed a man until last night. It was more fun than I thought it would be. Maybe I'll start branching out. There's many people out there who need to be freed, Tessa. You should be honored that you get to be one of them."

This man was on a whole other level of sick and twisted, and I didn't need to hear another word out of his horrible mouth. Somehow, I knew that there was no reasoning behind his killings other than what lived in his mind, and I didn't want to know what his brain contained. I tightened my grip on Finn's harness. She was as tense as a bowstring, ready to fly at this man, to protect me with her life. I couldn't let her do that. Somehow, I had to get us out of this situation.

Scott rolled his shoulders as he stared at me.

"What? Cat got your tongue? Speaking of cats, yours is gonna pay for this," he said, pointing at his cheek. "I can't decide if I want to make you watch or do that later, so I can really take my time. What do you think, Tessa? You've got options. It's the least I can do."

I needed to keep him talking while I figured a way out of this mess. There was no way I'd let him harm a hair on either of my pet's heads.

"I have options? Fine. Let them go. Both of them. Why do you do it, Scott? I'm trying to understand your need to kill innocent people. What are you freeing them from?"

He raised a hand and shook his finger at me.

"I'm not an idiot, Tessa. I know what you're doing. You're thinking you can stall for time while you pump me for information and wait for me to be distracted so you can make your move. Well, you know what happens when someone tries to get one up on me? Bad things, Tessa Windsor. Terrible things."

He kicked out, towards where Briar was hiding behind the wheel of the Land Rover, and she yowled, a horrible sound that made my heart stop. I didn't think. I didn't plan. I just reacted. My hand came up, almost of its own volition, and I reached for Scott Trager, fingers curled.

"Stop!"

I didn't even recognize the sound of my voice. It was deeper, more resonant. Light flared around me as I watched, amazed, as Scott froze in place, foot still extended. I stared at my hand as my fingers made a fist. He toppled over, still in the same position, his face pulled into a rictus of fear.

"Finally! Why did you wait so long to do that?" Briar asked as she strolled out from underneath the vehicle, tail held high.

"Wait? What? I'm doing this? What's happening?"

Panic laced my words, and my voice sounded like mine again.

"You commanded him to stop. Now, be quick, I don't know how long the magic will hold. We've got to get him tied up and call the police," Briar said, hopping into the back of the Land Rover and rummaging through the box held by the netting on the side panel. "Don't you have ropes back here?"

Finn gave a soft woof and stared up at me, her brown eyes wide.

"You did it. I knew you would. Are you okay? Your face is all bruised."

"Now, people," Briar said, shooting us an exasperated glance. "We need rope. Talk later. Tie up the creepy serial killer first."

I felt like I was in slow motion as I walked to the Land Rover. Finn leaned against my leg, never taking her eyes off the man at our feet. She whined and her voice held a panicky note.

"Hurry, I think he's waking up."

I wrenched the box out of the netting and dumped it out, scattering the contents everywhere. I had carabiners, bungee cords, and random odds and ends. I grabbed the cords and knelt.

"If I can get them tight enough, these will work."

Scott was still frozen, but his eyes were alert as I moved his arms, bringing them together. I shuddered at the expression visible in those depths and worked as fast as I could, wrapping the cord around his wrists until it dented into his skin. I pulled as hard as I could and fastened the two ends together in the front, where his fingers couldn't reach.

"His ankles! Quick!"

I used the second cord and wrapped his feet together as Briar shouted at me.

"He's moving his fingers!"

I finished and stepped back, searching around for my pack. I needed my phone and my gun and both were inside of it. Scott blinked, slowly, ever so slowly, and my heart nearly stopped.

"Where's my pack? What did he do with it?"

"His car," Finn said, breaking away, her lead trailing behind her as she raced across the parking lot. "I didn't leave you when you fell, but he carried it over here."

She pawed at the door, but the sound of an engine drowned out the rest of her words as a familiar pickup plowed into the lot, skidding to a stop next to me.

Burt Quinlan stepped out, pistol held steady as he pointed it at the man I'd trussed up like a turkey.

"Well, would you look at that? I'm sure glad I listened to my gut and came back. What's going on here?"

"He's a killer," I said as Finn came skittering back, her tail held low as she stared at Burt. "He was going to kill all of us. He hid until you left."

Briar stared at Burt from her spot in the back of the Land Rover and he nodded in her direction.

"I've got him, cat. Don't you worry. Call the cops, Miss Tessa. I've got you covered."

I jogged over to Scott's car and wrenched open the door, finding my pack on the front seat. I pulled my phone out of the pack and dialed Jace's number. It rang twice before his irritated voice came on the line.

"What now? You've got another hobo I need to talk to?"

"Shut up, Jace. Just shut your mouth. I am not in the mood for this. I just caught your killer. He tried to kill me, along with Finn and Briar. We're at the Prism Lake trailhead. Send as many units as you can. Hurry!"

I ended the call before I could rip into him any further and Burt blinked at me, while Scott groaned on the ground.

"Well, that's one way to call the cops. I take it you two know each other?"

"You could say that. Thanks for coming back, Burt. You saved us."

He chuckled, shaking his head.

"Looks to me like you can take care of yourself just fine. How did you overpower him? Got him just right?"

I couldn't reveal to Burt that I strongly suspected I'd used magic to save us. I wasn't entirely sure how I'd done it. So, I said the first thing that came to my mind.

"Something like that."

Finn's ears perked as she stared towards the road. I almost asked her what she heard before remembering Burt was right there. Seconds later, though, I heard a beautiful sound. Sirens. And they weren't too far away. I relaxed a fraction.

"They're coming. There must have been a deputy close by."

Burt nodded as Scott Trager shifted his position, his eyes full of murder as they stared at me, ignoring the man holding a gun on him.

"Uh, this guy ain't right, is he?"

"No, Burt. Not one bit."

"You stay put, you hear?" Burt said, never moving his pistol from Scott's face. "I don't take kindly to men who rough up women, let alone kill them. I won't hesitate to blow you away."

Scott made a groaning sound and moved, but the cords I'd tied held. I turned and used both arms to wave as a sheriff's department car turned off the highway.

"Right here. He's over here."

The car pulled in behind Burt's pickup and a young deputy got out, service weapon drawn. He looked between Burt and the man on the ground, like he wasn't certain which one was the biggest threat.

"The man tied up is Scott Trager. He killed Felicity, and he tried to kill me. Kill all of us. Burt's helping me."

The deputy nodded and approached, his voice surprisingly calm given how young he looked.

"Backup is on the way. Stop moving, sir. That's an order."

More sirens sounded, and I called Finn to my side, picking up her trailing lead. Briar sat in the back of the Land Rover, still growling faintly at every movement Trager made.

"Which one of you tied him up?" The deputy asked.

Burt shot me a grin filled with pride and nodded in my direction.

"Miss Tessa did that. Looks like she got those cords right and tight."

A faint bloom of pride swelled my chest, forcing the fear back into a corner, where it sat crouched, still not willing to believe it was all over. Two more squad cars rocketed into the lot and a door flung open. Jace Roberts moved faster than I'd ever seen him move, even when he played on the defensive line in college.

"Alright men, we've got him," he said, moving in and hauling Trager to his feet with a rough jerk. "Cuff him and stuff him."

Two other deputies swarmed over and clasped cuffs and shackles on Trager, who was standing there, eerily silent, his eyes never leaving my face. My stomach rolled at the expression, but I refused to back down. He hadn't beaten me. I wasn't helpless.

"He killed Art Callahan. I think you'll find his body in the woods on the Ridgeline Trail. I can help look for him," I said, as they marched Trager over to a squad car, a deputy on each side of him.

Burt holstered his weapon and held out his hand to Jace.

"Burt Quinlan."

"Jace Roberts. What department are you in?"

Burt's smile peeked out from underneath that bushy mustache.

"I'm retired, but I was with the Dallas County sheriff's office back in the day. You're good at spotting a fellow officer."

"Well, thank you Quinlan. Your quick thinking saved the day."

Burt cleared his throat and shook his head, flashing me a smile as his eyes crinkled up in the corners.

"No sir. That honor goes to Miss Tessa here. She had him trussed up by the time I came back. Had a bad feeling about that guy. They say cop instincts never go away, and I guess they're right."

Jace looked at me, finally truly looked at me, and his forehead bunched into lines as his eyes strayed over my cheek.

"Tessa..."

"I'm fine," I said, hand straying to what felt like a spectacular bruise on my cheek. "Thank you for coming so quickly."

Our dislike faded into something that, while not entirely comfortable, was at least not as adversarial. He nodded and adjusted his duty belt.

"You're sure about him killing Art?"

I nodded and stared at my shoes as sorrow swamped my senses.

"I'm certain. He had no reason to lie. As far as he knew, I wouldn't live long enough to do anything with that information."

"How did you... I mean... I don't get it."

I shrugged and squinted at him.

"Got lucky I guess. I can take care of myself."

"That you can, Miss Tessa. That you can. I'd be honored to help with the search for the other man he killed, Deputy Roberts. The wife isn't expecting me back until tonight, and I've got time," Burt volunteered.

"I can come, too," I said, wrapping Finn's lead around my hand. "Finn and Briar can help."

Jace shook his head.

"No, Tessa. You need to get to the hospital and get that cheek looked at. We'll take it from here. I'm going to need to interview you, but that can wait until later. I called your brother right after you called me. He's on his way."

Who was this man and what had he done with Jace Roberts? It was the kindest he'd ever been to me. Somehow, it didn't feel right.

"I'll be fine. I want to help."

"Now, Miss Tessa, I think you've done enough for one day," Burt said, his hand gentle as he touched my arm. "I don't think you need to see any more nastiness today. You might feel okay right now, but as soon as that adrenaline wears off, you're gonna need to take a break. Trust me. You're a strong woman, but you've done enough. We'll take it from here."

My lips felt quivery as I tried to smile at Burt, so I bit down on the bottom one to contain my emotions.

"Okay."

Finn woofed, and I turned to see Paul's pickup skidding on the highway as he negotiated the sharp turn onto the trailhead. I glimpsed his pale face as he threw open the door and ran towards me, arms open wide. Everything I'd been holding back came crashing forward as the floodgates to my emotions opened. Paul wrapped his arms around me and kept the pieces together, while Finn leaned against my leg. A soft paw scratched at my other leg, and I bent down to scoop up Briar, holding her close to my chest as tears streamed down my cheeks.

Paul's voice shook as he stepped back and touched my cheek with a finger.

"My God, Tessa. What happened?"

I wanted to answer, but words failed me. Luckily, Burt stepped up to the plate and filled him in on the basics. The rest? That would have to wait until later. All that mattered was that Scott Trager was behind bars, where he belonged. He wouldn't kill again.

Chapter Twenty-Two

A soft breeze fluttered along the edges of the awning that shaded us, and the gravesite, from the sun. Paul and Meggie stood on either side of me, both unwilling to let me out of their sight after the events of a few days ago. No other mourners had joined us for Art Callahan's funeral, or the burial, but I took some small shred of comfort since he wasn't entirely alone.

Paul and I had paid for the ceremony, and the headstone that sat above Art's last resting place, right next to our family plot. We'd tried to find out if Art had any living relatives and had come up empty. So, we unofficially adopted him as part of our family. Finn laid down next to the headstone, her brown eyes filled with sadness. Briar book ended her on the other side of the stone, head drooping down as they both paid their respects.

The pastor had already left. The grave had been filled in, but none of us were in any hurry to leave Art behind. I knelt next to Finn and traced the carving of the Labrador Retriever we'd asked to be added to the stone. I knew little about Art, but he'd mentioned his dog, Jimmy, and it had felt right to include his old buddy.

Paul's hand gripped my shoulder.

"You okay, sis?"

I nodded and stood, brushing off my skirt. Okay was a pretty relative term, and I was still coming to grips with what happened. Nightmares stalked my sleep, replaying what could have happened if my magic hadn't worked. I didn't understand it. But each day that passed, I found it a little easier to get up and go about my day. I mourned a man I'd barely known, and now we were finally laying him to rest. I heaved a sigh and forced a smile.

"Yeah. Or I guess it's better to say I will be. Thanks for coming with us, Megs. It means a lot."

"Of course. I'm sorry about Art. I never met him, but I'm glad we could be here for him. At least it's a beautiful day."

She was right. It had been gloomy over the past three days, in more ways than one, but today, the sun was shining and life was moving on. I wouldn't forget Art Callahan, or Felicity. People I'd never truly known, but somehow, our lives had intertwined.

"Ready to go?" I asked, picking up Finn's lead.

Briar stood and walked around the headstone with careful paws, coming to a stop at my feet. She blinked her beautiful green eyes.

"Thank you for letting us come. I know the pastor thought it was strange, but we really wanted to be here."

I scooped her up and pressed a kiss on her tiny head.

"Of course. We're all family."

We straggled back to our vehicles, each of us lost in thought. I still couldn't believe that a week ago, I'd received that mysterious letter, which had kicked off a whirlwind that landed us here, at the Collinsville cemetery.

"Are you guys hungry?" Meggie asked, giving me a gentle smile as I stopped at the Land Rover. "We could head to the restaurant and I'll make you guys some lunch."

Meggie's love language was definitely feeding people. She'd shown up at my cabin, after Paul brought me home, following the capture of Scott Trager, her arms full of grocery bags. She'd stayed with me for the first two nights, making sure I ate properly, crashing on the couch so I wouldn't be alone with my thoughts. Or my nightmares. She was the best friend I could ever ask for.

Paul had perked up as visions of one of Meggie's famous green chile burgers, likely danced in his head, but I shook my head.

"I'm okay. You two go ahead. There are a few things I need to do."

Paul sobered and frowned, and I didn't miss the worried glance he shared with Meggie. They'd played tag-team mother-hens for the past few days, never leaving me alone for longer than it took for me to use the bathroom.

"Seriously, guys, I'm fine," I said, smiling at both of them. "Have lunch. Besides, I thought we were gonna get your stuff moved later on, right? You'll need fuel to get all those boxes of books moved into your new home. Go have lunch and I'll meet you both at the apartment in a few hours."

Paul had delayed the big move in the aftermath, but it was clear he was itching to be in his new home. His lease was ending in two weeks, and the clock was ticking to get his apartment cleaned out.

"We're crowding you, aren't we?" Meggie asked, flashing me a grin. "I can tell you're chafing. We just... Well, we care, Tessa. We almost lost you."

"It's not that. There's just something I want to do by myself. I'll meet up with you both later. I promise. Besides, you can fit a lot of books in the back of this bad boy," I said, slapping the side of the Land Rover.

"Alright," Paul said, before pressing a kiss to the side of my head. "But if you need anything, you'll call, right?"

"Of course. Go. Eat. I'm just not hungry right now."

"I'll bring some food with me for later," Meggie said. "You need to keep up your strength, Tess."

"Sounds good. See you two later."

With hesitant steps, they trailed off to their respective vehicles. I waved as they pulled out of the parking lot, one after the other, and turned to face Finn.

"You two ready for this?"

Finn wagged her plumed tail and gave me a doggy grin.

"Of course. Let's go!"

Briar squiggled in my grasp and I let her down as we headed

back to the cemetery. I'd done a little research and discovered that our great aunt Euphemia had been buried in this cemetery, far away from the plot we'd just visited. I'd debated telling Paul, but there was something I needed to do, and this time, I wanted to do it alone. I'd tell him about it later, and maybe we could visit again, together. Or he could go by himself if he wanted to.

We followed the paved path through the cemetery, and I noted the sections as we walked.

"Why do you think she picked a spot clear over here?" Briar asked as she kept pace with Finn.

"I don't know. I guess, I mean, obviously, there were issues with my dad's side of the family, but it's sad to think those would carry on, even after she was gone. Maybe there's another reason."

We reached the right section and began walking down the line of stones, looking for the right one. I recognized none of the names, but finally, we reached hers, sitting next to a giant blue spruce.

"Maybe this explains it," I said, looking around. "It's peaceful over here. And that is a gorgeous tree. It's got to be at least a hundred years old. It's enormous!"

Finn wagged her tail slowly as I knelt down next to the stone with my great aunt's name on it. I traced the carving of her name and marshaled my thoughts. There was so much I wanted to say.

"Euphemia," I said, softly. "I wish I'd known you. I have so many questions, and nowhere to turn. I'm going to keep reading your diaries, though. I may be wrong, but I think you helped me. I think it was your voice telling me to get up. The magic you gave me saved us. There just aren't the right words to say everything that's in my heart, but thank you. Thank you for saving us."

Tears clogged in my throat, and my vision went blurry as I sat under the shade of the giant tree. Finn leaned against my shoulder and Briar snuggled into my lap as we bowed our heads in honor of a woman we'd never met.

A bit of wind kicked up, and for a moment, it felt like someone brushed a kiss onto the bruise that was healing on my cheek. I cupped my hand over it as tears continued to fall. Finn let out a low whine and dipped her head.

"Thank you," I whispered.

Slowly, my tears stopped and my cheeks dried, but still we sat, feeling Euphemia's presence all around us. I hadn't touched her diary since the events at Prism Lake, but I couldn't wait to get back to it. Maybe, either in that volume, or one of the older ones, I'd find some answers. But right now, it was enough to know that she'd been there. She'd helped me. I believed that with every fiber of my being. I rubbed my eyes and stood, still cradling my cat.

"All right, guys. Let's head back. I'd better get you back to the cabin and get some lunch for you."

Finn wagged, and her tongue lolled out in a cheerful grin.

"I'm glad we came here. Maybe we can come back sometime. I'd like to visit Euphemia again."

I glanced back at the grave, shadowed by the spruce tree, and nodded.

"I'd like that. Maybe she would, too."

For a split second, I caught sight of something shimmering above her headstone, but it was gone by the time I blinked. I shook my head and kept walking.

"At least we'll finally have the cabin to ourselves. I appreciate what Meggie and Paul have been doing, but it will be nice to have some space. The past few days have felt like we've been suspended in goo. It's time to get back to living our lives again."

Briar purred and kneaded my arm with her paws, her claws brushing my skin.

"I like the sound of that. When is our next hike?"

Finn gave me a hopeful look as she jogged next to me. My pets enjoyed my job almost as much as I did. Sometimes, maybe even a little more. I chuckled and reached down to stroke her head.

"Well, we rescheduled a few, so it's gonna be pretty busy for the next week. After that, we've got a nighttime camping hike on the books. I think that one's gonna be pretty fun. We don't do many of those."

"Don't forget to bring the sleeping pad," Briar said, her tone full of mischief. "I remember what happened the last time you did."

My back remembered, too. I'd quickly learned that after you hit thirty, the ground gets exponentially harder each year.

"I'll bring it. It should be an interesting one. An astronomy club from Denver booked the event. I guess there's a big meteor shower on that date, and we'll be heading to a spot on a mountain where the views should be amazing."

"Oh, that sounds like fun. Nice and peaceful," Finn said, wagging her tail as we neared the Land Rover. "That is exactly what we need after all of this excitement."

Briar yawned widely, showing me the back of her little pink throat.

"I hear that. A nice, calm event will be just the ticket."

I got everyone stowed in the vehicle and pulled out of the parking spot, feeling settled for the first time in days. My life had been upended, but so much good had come out of it. Now I could talk to my best friends. And hear their beautiful voices back. The magic within me had helped us catch a killer. And now, who knows what the future would hold? One thing was certain, I had a feeling it was going to be a wild ride.

Don't Miss A Guide to Uncovering Secrets

Tessa Windsor thought an overnight hike shepherding a group of astronomers to witness a meteor shower would be a peaceful, fun outing. But when Marcus Gallagher—the newly hired photographer for her brother's newspaper—tags along to capture the event, Tessa's nerves start to fray.

With her loyal border collie, Finn, and her clever cat, Briar, by her side, she's prepared for a dazzling display of stars mirrored in the serene lake where the group will camp. But when a fellow hiker —the astronomy club's leader—is found dead in the water the next morning, the trip takes a chilling turn.

Tessa is no stranger to solving mysteries with the help of her newfound magical powers and her talking animal companions, but this case is different. The group is filled with clashing personalities and hidden secrets, making it hard to know who to trust. Even Marcus seems rattled by the rising tension. As sparks fly between Marcus and Tessa, so do questions about who could have turned a peaceful night into a nightmare.

With Finn's boundless loyalty, Briar's sharp instincts, and Marcus's keen eye for detail, Tessa must untangle a web of motives before the killer strikes again. Can she uncover the truth hidden among the stars, or will the darkness claim another victim?

Books By Courtney McFarlin

A Razzy Cat Cozy Mystery Series

The Body in the Park

The Trouble at City Hall

The Crime at the Lake

The Thief in the Night

The Mess at the Banquet

The Girl Who Disappeared

Tails by the Fireplace

The Love That Was Lost

The Problem at the Picnic

The Chaos at the Campground

The Crisis at the Wedding

The Murder on the Mountain

The Reunion on the Farm

The Mishap at the Meeting

The Bones on the Trail

The Dispute at the Fair

The Commotion at the Race

The Spy in the Sand - Coming in Spring 2025

A Soul Seeker Cozy Mystery

The Apparition in the Attic

The Banshee in the Bathroom

The Creature in the Cabin

The ABCs of Seeing Ghosts

The Demon in the Den

The Ether in the Entryway

The Fright in the Family Room

The Ghoul in the Garage

The Haunting in the Hallway

The Imp at the Ice Rink

The Jinn in the Joists

The Kelpie in the Kennel

The Lady in the Library

The Manifestation in the Mansion - Coming in Spring 2025

The Clowder Cats Cozy Mystery Series

Resorting to Murder

A Slippery Slope

A Mountain of Mischief

Pushing Up Daisies

A Taste of Trouble - Coming Spring of 2025!

Millie the Miracle Cat Cozy Mystery Series

A New Beginning

Stacked Against Us

Volumes of Lies

The Poison Pen - Early Summer 2025

NEW! Finn and Briar Cozy Mystery Series

A Guide to Solving a Murder

A Guide to Uncovering Secrets - Summer of 2025

A Siren's Song Paranormal Cozy Mystery Series

The Wrong Note

A Major Case

The Missing Beat - Early 2025

Escape from Reality Cozy Mystery Series

Escape from Danger

Escape from the Past

Escape from Hiding

A Note From Courtney

Thank you for taking the time to read this novel. If you enjoyed the book, please take a few minutes to leave a review. As an independent author, I appreciate the help!

If you'd like to be first in line to hear about new books as they are released, don't forget to sign up for my newsletter. Click here to sign up! https://bit.ly/2H8BSef

A Little About Me

Courtney McFarlin currently lives in the Black Hills of South Dakota with her fiancé and their two cats.

Find out more about her books at:
   www.booksbycourtney.com

Follow Courtney on Social Media:

https://twitter.com/booksbycourtney

https://www.instagram.com/courtneymcfarlin/

https://www.facebook.com/booksbycourtneym

Printed in Great Britain
by Amazon